FOR BETTER

OR WORSE

BY: ANDREW BETHEL

To the readers:

Thank you for starting this journey with me, and taking a chance on my first official project. Once you reach the end, I can guarantee you won't be disappointed. Thus, I hope to see you continue to ride with me from series to series, and grow into the future. Much love and blessings.

FOR BETTER

OR WORSE

By: Andrew Bethel

1

"Look Out!" J Bug cut the wheel to the left, just nearly avoiding colliding into a car in front of them. As sparks flew off the side of the car, he smashed his foot even harder on the pedal. The stolen 2015 Aston Martin Vantage lurched forward as the needle cruised past eighty. "They still on us?" Break turned his head to check behind him, and located the two squad cars cutting around the same vehicle behind them.

"Hell yeah they still there, push this muthafucka my nigga!" J Bug ain't even bother responding as he focused back on the road, and getting away. Break rolled down his window, stuck his .380 out, and started making it bark at the closest car. Holes appeared in the windshield, and a few bounced off the front grill, but it was his last loaded bullet that found its home inside the front left tire. The squad car tipped, then swerved into the bumper off a vehicle in the next lane. The angle it hit sent the car in the air and spinning.

"Oohh shit nigga, Haha, did you see that shit!" He celebrated. "Yeah nice, now do it again, until they all gone, and shut the fuck up so I can focus!" Break looked sideways at Bug and shot him the middle finger. Bug took his hand off the wheel long enough to return one, as Break reloaded and did what his boy suggested.

Leaning out the window, he sent two more shots flying in the direction of the new squad car in the lead. He almost flew out the window when Bug had to swerve around another car, but he quickly regained his composure holding on tighter to the 'Oh

Shit' bar. He steadied his burner as much as he could and aimed for the windshield.

He had taken out the last car, but this one he was playing for keeps. His first shot went a little high, but the next one hit its mark head on. The head of the officer snapped back, and the car swerved left then hard right into a roll. A red Toyota Camry got caught in its path, getting propelled into the back rear of a Chevy Suburban.

A chain reaction of automobile chaos continued until there was a wall of disabled vehicles in the pile-up, blocking the road. "Yeeeaaahhh, Fuck the police you weak ass bitches!" He celebrated damn near dancing out of the window onto the roof. Bug couldn't help but laugh at his day one partner's antics, "Mayne get yo ass back in this window 'for some Final Destination shit happen to you." He grabbed his leg and yanked him in for emphasis. "Mayne fuck death nigga, did you see that? I am the reaper." That nigga got to posin like there was paparazzi around or something, before he cranked the music up and settled back into his seat.

2

Ten Minutes later they were pulling into Big Mike's junk-yard. They rode around back and parked inside the open waiting garage. As usual, the door began closing the second they passed under it. Big Mike appeared as they were hopping out, "What the fuck is all them scratches on the side of it!?" J Bug looked at Break and rolled his eyes, "What's up guys, how ya'll doin, glad to see ya'll made it safe. You know, something like that would be nice."

Mike scrunched up his nose, "Nigga save dat shit for ya bitch, this is strictly business." "Yeah well business got a lit-tle crazy today, and that shit there is collateral damage." Break jumped in, "Hell yeah, you shoulda seen ya boi. We had cars flip-pin and spinnin on some Fast & Furious shit. It was a narrow escape, but them fuck bois couldn't match up in the end." He stated proudly.

"Nigga dis ain't no muthafuckin movie, and look what you did to the product." Big Mike reached into a bag and pulled a couple stacks out of it before tossing the bag at their feet. "The fuck you removing bands for, after all the shit we went through to get this here. It was hot as hell from the jump, you should be addin stacks if anything." Break snatched the bag off the floor heatedly.

The whole time J Bug just stood there quietly. He was barely paying attention to the exchange. They had been doing this for almost 20 years, and never had he felt suspect about anything. At the moment though, he was feeling all kinds of wrong. Something was off, his instincts were screaming at him, and he didn't like what they were telling him.

"Yo fuck it Break, it's all good. Let's get up out of here." Knowin his mans like the back of his hand, he picked up on his uneasiness. "Aight you got this one Mike, but next time show some muthafuckin love!" With that, they dipped out and got in a car waiting for them in the parking lot. "What's good bruh, you straight?" Break stared at his boy with a look of concern painted on his face. Bug was still a little spaced trying to shake the feeling, but it just seemed to get worse.

It wasn't until they were down the road that he understood why. The red & blue lights dancing in the rear-view mirror damn near sent his heart into his chest. Before he could even completely pull over, six other squad cars appeared out of nowhere and surrounded them. "Step out of the vehicle and put your hands in the air, you try anything funny and we'll light your ass up!" Break instinctively reached for his burner, but Bug stayed his hand. "J Bug... Break... don't make this hard. Get out of the vehicle NOW!" At the mention of their names, they knew the deal. "Fuck bruh... somebody set us up!"

3

13 Years Later

"Gabryiana get yo ass up! If you get suspended for missing another day of school, I'ma beat the black off ya... and I guarantee you'll make a funny lookin ass white person." Baby G kicked the covers off her frustrated, and pounded her fist on the bed, "Argh fuck school." She muttered sleepily. "What was that you said little girl?!" "Uh-nothin, I said yes ma'am I'm coming!" she yelled in the sweetest voice she could muster up. "That's what I thought you said, now hurry up."

She rose out of her bed and walked zombie like to her closet. (I swear she got hearing like a jungle cat or something.) She thought. She wiped the sleep from her eyes as she took in her figure in her full-sized mirror on her closet door. Even though she was only 15. Her body had curves that were killing most grown women. She was 5'2 with honeyish caramel complexion, hazel eyes, and long natural hair.

She chose a fit out of the closet, and shimmied into some Baby Phat jeans that hugged her ass just right. Then tossed on her matching shirt, before jumping into a pair of her 33 J's. After hittin her hair and hygiene, she came stomping down the stairs. "Girl you best ta pick up your feet, I don't see no marching band round here. Breakfast is on the table, hurry up and eat, then get yo butt up to that school before the tardy bell rings. Not one single pit stop, and stay away from them little knuckleheaded friends you always getting in trouble behind."

Baby G brushed past her mom into the kitchen. "Did you hear me?" Her mother's eyes were focused on her as she stood arms crossed and foot tappin. "Yes Ma'am." She relented, knowing if she didn't, a swift hand would probably knock her on her ass. "Now that's better. I gotta get back to work, I only took an hour break to make sure you were up and good for the day. I know its tough baby girl, and I'm even tougher on you, but it's just because I love you and want the best for you. Your so damn smart and I know you can do anything if you just put your mind to it, but you gotta choose the right things. Not what you've been choosing to do out in them streets. You all I got baby, and I don't want you ending up a caged animal like your father."

Baby G softened a little at her mother's words. She knew they rang true and understood where she was coming from. Sometimes she even felt bad for the pain she be putting her through, but life wasn't as simple as she made it sound. Plus, the streets were full of opportunities, and she was ready to seize em all. That paper wasn't gonna make itself for shit sure.

"I understand mama, I'll try and do better." She said instead. "That's my baby girl. Now come give mama some love before I gotta get back to work with the savages." A hug & kiss later, and she was finally alone in the house. She finished scarfing down her breakfast, then pulled her Iphone out and dialed a

number, "Pull up." Was all she said before she hung up.

Sure that enough time had passed where her mother

hadn't forgotten something and doubled back, she ran upstairs

to her room. She pulled her backpack from under the bed and

checked inside. Everything was as she had left it, like she sus-

pected. She pulled out her baby nina, and double checked the

clip. Then she threw on her hoodie, threw the bag on her back

and skipped a few steps down the stairs.

She stepped outside just in time to see Skiddlez coming

down the block wit the system knockin. By time she had locked

the door, his '87 Chevy Caprice on 28"s was pullin up in front.

Candy coated in tropical blue from the skittles packet, with the

interior yellow, orange, to red like a sunset, he sat idling by the

curb waiting for her to hop in. When she did, she looked at him

as he was rolling up the wake N' bake, "You find him?"

He took his eyes off the sweet long enough to answer, "Yeah

Trackz was on that nigga, said he ran his bitch ass into the school and into first period. Ol' simp ass nigga was the only one in the class with the teacher helping her set up the room and shit." Then he dropped his focus back on to the task in his hands. "School huh? That's cool, I made a promise to go there today anyways." She laughed at the irony. "Tell the squad I hope everybody did they homework, because we attendin in full today atleast until lunch."

Skiddlez nodded his head as he sparked the blunt, then started shootin the texts out to the squad. They sat in the front of the crib hot boxin and plottin for a minute, before they pulled off in the direction of the school house. When they pulled into the parking lot, they stunted their way over to the normal area to meet, when they actually decided to attend school.

Jo-Jo was already there with his arms wrapped around his girl Gina. Roscoe was leaned up against his Tahoe with his brother Ant, choppin it up wit Trackz. When they pulled up every one's eyes were locked on em. Trackz smiled, then you could see his lighter spark as he lit up the stick he had been holding until they arrived.

They parked sideways next to him blocking the road and hopped out, leaving the doors open so the knock could spread through the parking lot as they dapped eachother up. The security guard was mugging, but they all turned and shot him the bird making him drop his head, then go on about his business somewhere else.

Earlier in the year he had made the mistake of tryna run up on em playing top flight security. They beat his ass every day for a month following until he finally got the hint that they weren't to be fucked with. They kicked the shit and passed the loud sticks round & round, drawing a crowd of people they knew, as they waited for the rest of the squad to get there.

The moment they were spotted they were on the clock, hand in hand servin half the school. Even a few teachers copped from them, though they always disguised it by making it look like they were lecturing them before secretly scoring and departing. Five minutes before the first bell rang, Ivory finally pulled up in his cocaine white Impala, followed by Prissy in her brand-new Pink Cadillac that her man D-Money bought her. Who of course, was also riding shotgun puffin on a big ass gorilla finger blunt stuffed wit some fire ass loud.

Seeing the squad in act, his fool ass leaned over and onto the horn actin a ass to announce their arrival as if everyone hadn't already seent and heard them coming. "Nigga why the fuck you ain't just push your own shit up here, instead of pulling up here like you was Pinky or something?" Skiddlez joked. "Cuz I ain't wanna take away from my baby flossin on everybody nigga, act like you know!" He emphasized by leaning over and givin Prissy a big juicy kiss.

"Aww nigga please, first of all you only bought that cuz you lazy as fuck and wanted my girl to drive you around like she yo chauffeur or something. And second, you know her joint way flyer than yours, so she'd a been shittin all over you not the other way around." Baby G spat, then her and Prissy high fived each other knowing it was the truth.

"Oh so it's like that?" He looked at Prissy with his hand over his heart feigning like he was hurt. They all bust out laughing at that, "So what's up wit that lil fuck boi Henry?" Roscoe asked on a more seious note, addressing the reason they were all there.

Baby G laced everybody up, first telling em what Trackz had relayed, then letting em know the plan. Everyone agreed, readied themselves, then broke off to their classes.

4

Soon as she got to first period, she lost interest. "So nice of you to grace us with your presence today Mrs. Hays." Her lame ass teacher joked upon seeing her. She went straight to her seat in the back corner, threw her headphones on, and leaned her head against the wall. Her teacher, used to her behavior, shook her head and got back to teaching the rest of the class.

What seemed like minutes later, one of the students were tapping her shoulder to wake her up, and let her know class was over. She chopped it up with the homies in the hallway to kill some time and not be the first one in class. That's when she spotted Henry. His eyes got wide when he spotted her too, and he took off running in the opposite direction like the bitch he was.

She couldn't do nothing but smile at his antics, then shot off to her next period. She sat down and went through the same routine she did in the first period.

When class ended, she shot a text to Skiddlez. A minute later she got her reply. [Boys bathroom, East hallway]. Immediately she headed away from the lunch crowd and in the direction of the target. The first thing she noticed when she walked in was the strong smell of piss.

"Damn, niggaz is so nasty. Do ya'll even aim for the toilet, or just walk in and piss all over the floor and walls?" She dapped up Roscoe and Ant who were standing guard at the door. Roscoe nodded his head around the corner, and she followed. She cleared the wall just in time to see Ivory's dark chocolate muscular 6' frame connect an uppercut to Henry.

"So, you thought school could save ya lil punk ass huh?" she said announcing her presence, "Obviously you ain't the brightest muthafucka, or you would have come up wit a better plan." He had the nerve to start crying, "Come on Baby G, please don't do this. I'm sorry, shit wasn't supposed to go down the way it did."

Trackz reacted by soccer kickin him straight in the gut, "Da fuck you mean nigga! You ain't mean to set the homie up, steal his package, and then drop a dirty ass dime to top it off?!" "Yeah, exactly which part wasn't supposed to go down the way it did, because from where we stand it all looked intentional." Jo-Jo mugged from the wall where his light skinned athletic build was posted up on.

Skiddlez was sitting in a stall on top of a closed toilet quietly watching everything. He looked at Baby G then held up a rolled stick with a questioning look. "Trackz, snatch that nigga shirt off and stuff it under the door." He did what she said, then she nodded at Skiddlez giving him the ok. He wasted no time sparking up. She lifted an eyebrow at D-Money and he got the hint.

"Yeah we checked him from head to toe. Threw his phone in the toilet after smashing it on the ground. Lil muthafucka ain't have nothing but $60 in his pockets. He tried to run twice already, that's why he's all fucked up like that." They knew to take extra precautions, because you can never trust a snitch.

She took the bleezy Skiddlez was handing her, squatted down in front of Henry, took a deep pull, then blew the cloud in his face. He began coughing uncontrollably. She slapped fire out his mouth, making the tears fall harder and snot drip from his nose, "Where the fuck is our money Henry?" He kept sniffling then cried harder. She back handed him, "Shut yo bitch ass up nigga, I asked you a question."

His eyes darted around the room at the squad. "Don't even think about it nigga, we WILL kill you if you try to run again. Heed the kindness your being offered, and answer the question." Skiddlez said through clenched teeth. He dropped his head, "I don't know, I don't have it." "Well it's obvious, you ain't have nothing but that funky ass $60 on you. So where did you put the rest?"

"It's gone... All of it." Baby G reached in her back pocket, and pulled out a switchblade, pushing the button as she brought it into view. She stuck him in his exposed belly just hard enough to break skin, and draw a trickle of blood. She scraped it up from his belly, across his chest, and to his throat. Her concentration was broken by a laugh from behind her. She narrowed her eyes and glared at Jo-Jo, "My bad, I just didn't know they still made them muthafuckas," He straightened up and tried to keep a straight face, "For real, my bad. It's the weed, this some good shit."

She rolled her eyes, and directed her attention back on her prey. She jabbed the knife harder into his Adam's apple. He looked down and she followed his gaze, then saw a puddle forming under him. She took a step back and looked at him incredulously, before backhanding him again. "I'm... I'm sorry..." he stuttered embarrassed.

She was growing more agitated by the minute, "Fuck that, what you mean it's all gone?" "I gave it all to the police." Sounds of disbelief filled the room. Ivory charged him, and stuck him with a two piece, "You expect us to believe you just handed damn near five racks over to the police?! Don't fuckin lie to us again!" He cocked back to deliver another, until Baby G poked his arm and shook her head. He fell back behind her breathing hard.

"We know they only caught you wit a zip Henry." "Yeah and that's all it took for yo weak ass to get to runnin your mouth." Skiddlez cut in. "From what you hit the homie for, we did the math, and there's five racks missing, so stop playing wit us before it's game over." She dug the knife deeper into his neck, to where a little bead of blood started forming.

"I swear on my mama, they asked me where the rest was and where I got it from. That if I told em everything, then they'd let me go. So I did." He said honestly. "You expect us to believe that dumb ass shit?" Trackz asked. "It's the truth, I swear it."

Baby G shook her head, "Let me get this straight. You set the homie up, hit his stash, got popped later without the work tryna slang a lil zip, snitch on the homie AND give up the info on where you stashed everything?!" He shook his head yes.

"So, you basically did all that fuckboi shit for nothing?" Jo-Jo stated disgusted. "Well not exactly nothing... I got my freedom AND I learned a valuable lesson." That was about all that Baby G could take. She jabbed him in the nose, when he opened his mouth to scream, she told Ivory to grab his tongue. He gladly grabbed it and damn near ripped it out of his mouth. Baby G followed up by stabbing the switchblade through the base of his tongue and slitting it down the middle till it came out the tip. Henry damn near bit off his tongue screaming. Ivory shoved it back in his mouth and covered it with his hand to stifle his cries.

"You gots to be the dumbest muthafucka I ever met. Since you wanna be a snake, I cut ya tongue like a serpent. If you tell a doctor to fix it, I'll just cut it again. You reap what you sow, and you pay what you owe. You got two weeks to give me my money, or I start cutting off body parts until you gotta slither on the ground like one.

You go to the police and get to running your mouth, and the president won't be able to stop me from taking ya life and every family member we can get our hands on. Do you fuckin understand me!?" He nodded his head yes. "I didn't hear you Henry!" "Yeth... Yeth I understand you." She signaled Ivory, and he hit him with the knockout punch.

"Drag him in the stall and clean him up so we can get out of here." She told the others while washing the blood off herself. "Skiddlez, meet me out by the whip in ten." Then she was heading out the door, her mind already focused on their next move. As chance would have it, two steps after the door closed behind her, she walked smack dab into the principle and the bitch ass security guard. The smell of the potent cannabis assaulted their noses before they actually layed eyes on her.

"Mrs. Hays, what a pleasant surprise." The principal said

with a smile that didn't touch his eyes. The security guard smirked then looked at the boy's restroom sign behind her, "Well that explains a lot. I wonder what other packages your hiding in that bag of yours." Before he could let anything else slick slip out his mouth, she sent her fist crashing into his abdomen. Caught off guard, he doubled over. The principal's smile faded, "I wish you hadn't done that. Larry, escort Mrs. Hays to my office immediately." She cut a look at him reminding him to keep his hands off, then turned and followed the principal to his office.

She thought about just taking off running, but figured what was the point. They'd probably just send the laws to her house, and she didn't want to have to bring her problems to her mother's doorstep. Alone with her in his office, Mr. Conley let out a long sigh. She looked at the worry lines on his face and salt & pepper hair.

"I just don't understand it Mrs. Hays. Your potential is off the charts, your grades show that you could be an honor student... When you actually decide to show up and participate.

Students look up to you, you could do so much with your life...

So why do you choose this?" He dumped the contents of her back

pack on his desk. Baggies of different narcotics tumbled onto it's

top, of all various sizes. He used his pocket square to reach in and

delicately remove the handgun.

She dropped her head, knowing she was in deep shit. He

shook his head, eyes scanning the items in front of them. "Being

unable to control your anger has put this situation out of my

hands. By now Larry has already contacted the authorities

about you blatantly putting your hands on him." "I thought ya'll

were the authorities." She said smartly.

He ignored her comment and continued. "A word of ad-

vice, if you don't get that temper under control soon. It'll be

your undoing like the majority of all African Americans from

povertized regions. Do you understand what I am telling your

Mrs. Hays?" He looked at her sternly.

He knew her story, and it hurt his heart seeing the direction her life was going. He took this job to make a different, but seemed to feel like it was a losing battle these days more often than not. It was like the kids were just giving up. Poisoned by technology, the media, and entertainment, education was becoming less and less a priority in the land of free.

Majority of them didn't realize they were marching to the beat of sovereign drums, right into the hands of the enemies, who had long disguised this well thought out miseducation. What happened to the revolution? Where did all the revolutionist go? He snapped back to the problem at hand. "Look, I can take most of this hard shit off your hands, and most definitely all of that good marijuana you came out the bathroom advertising..."

He paused for effect letting a genuine smile escape. She looked at him dumbstruck, and let a slither of hope enter. "... but your gonna have to own up to this gun, because personally I don't know the dirt you've done with it and I'm not willing to take that risk. Do you understand what I'm telling you?" She nodded her head and let it drop back down. "Pick your head up!

If your going to choose the actions then you must face the con-sequences with confidence and strength. You stand behind the choices you make, especially the mistakes. You learn from and use them as guides to make things positive. Always with your head up..."

He picked the ounces of weed up and threw them in a drawer, then did the same with the ecstasy and powder. "I'm not touching the crack or the heroin because I don't believe in the history of the effects they've had on our people. Now with what you got left, there's a high probability that your going off to Juvie.

Listen to what I am telling you young lady. DO NOT let them break you, and DO NOT let this make you a statistic. Use your time wisely and think out every step of the way from here. No matter what anybody tells you, you CAN do ANYTHING you put your mind to. So, hold your head up and put your mind to something great Mrs. Hayes."

It was then that the real authorities came through the door and apprehended her. Much went through her mind as she went through the process of getting violated, charged, booked, and convicted. Even more as she was thrown into her new filthy and hostile environment. Though her pride didn't let her tell the principle at the time. She was grateful for what he had done and said, and most importantly, every word he spoke to her that day stuck.

5

"Tasha, where the fuck's my SIG at?" "It should be in the same spot it always is, in between the Beretta and the Choppa!" She yelled from the kitchen. Skiddlez stared at the empty slot, in the hidden bookshelf gun safe, frustrated and confused. "Well it ain't, so where the fuck is it?!" The sound of a pan slamming was followed by stomping footsteps coming down the hall. Tasha's petite frame come storming into the room wearing nothing but a T-Shirt and her panties. She didn't have much ass, but there was just enough to jiggle with every stomping step.

She pushed him out of the way and looked at the empty space and sucked her teeth. She snaked her micro braided hair in his direction and rolled her eyes before walking over to the closet. "Now see, this the shit I be talkin about. You come in here covered in dirt throwed out ya damn mind late in the night, and don't even put shit where it's supposed to be Tommy."

She reached in the bottom of the closet and pulled a body armor vest with the SIG rifle he was looking for stuffed in it. "Now what if the po-lice woulda came in here, after God knows what you did, lookin for evidence. You'da damn sho made that one easy as hell for em huh? That shit was sloppy, and we both know you better than that."

He hung his head sheepishly as the memory of the night before came flashing back. His usual connects had been giving him the run around all day with that "The shipment's around the corner" bull-shit. After 8 hours of missing big money, he went looking elsewhere which he hated doing. There was this guy that had been tryna get them to fuck wit him for months, so he had Trackz reach out and set it up. He needed a ride to the spot and ended up bringin a homeboy. When they got to the apartment complex, he said the guy didn't like meeting new people and to give him the money and he'll run up and get it.

Now this went against everything Skiddlez was taught, but he was in a rush and sick of waiting. The promise of him leaving his homeboy in the car as collateral, eased his mind as well. After twenty minutes went by, the instincts he had been trying to ignore finally got his attention. They searched the apartments high and low, blowing up his phone the whole while. When it started going straight to voicemail, they knew the deal.

Heated, with no product, and now missing the re-up money, all attention turned on the collateral turned hostage. Unfortunate for him his life got played by what he thought was his homie, for a little bit of chump change. He didn't know where the plug stayed or where his boy had gone. He begged and pleaded all the way to the grave, that he was forced to dig, but the rage inside of Skiddlez wouldn't be calmed by anything less than a life. He was more pissed at himself than anything, his uncle had schooled him better than that, but somebody had to pay one way or another.

He had popped a few pills and downed a bottle at Trackz's house, then must've blacked out until recently waking up in his bed. "Helllooo!" Tasha snapped him out of his thoughts. "I asked you what the fuck happened anyways?" "Nothing baby, just a lack in judgement leadin to me havin to handle some business."

He tried to wrap his arms around her and go for a kiss, but she ducked out of his reach. "Ewww boy, hell naw wit yo dirty ass. Go take a damn shower, and you can wash them clothes and the sheets you muddied up ya damn self as well." She stuck her tongue out and headed back to the kitchen where the savory smell of bacon and eggs was coming from.

He looked down at himself, then at the bed realizing they were both covered in dirt and shook his head. "Aight you got that one." Was all he could say knowing he tripped out. Once he got fresh, he joined Tasha at the table where she had a pile of bacon, omelets, pancakes, and OJ waiting for him. This time she let him embrace her in a hug and kiss.

"Thank you baby, what would I do without you?" he whispered in her ear. "Probably be a nasty ass good for nothing nigga like most of ya homebois. Now you gonna tell me what's been up wit you the past couple days or what?" Her eyes bore into him waiting for an answer. "It's nothin really. I just been tryna make sure everything is perfect for Baby G when she comes home, and this bullshittin ass plug been fuckin shit up."

It had been three years since that incident had happened with Baby G getting locked up, and tonight she was finally coming home. Three years locked up, never droppin a single name, and the squad made sure to keep money on her books while holdin shit down on the outside. Skiddlez never stepped foot back into that school again after that day, or any other school for that matter.

He was third generation in the streets, and the oldest in the squad. His pops had got killed when he was 3, and his uncle had preened him for the family business from then. The loss of his father sent his mother to the pipe, so there was never any interference from her. Still, he liked to play the back ground and be a ghost.

Baby G on the other hand, loved the attention and the power. Which is why he gladly let her be the leader of the crew, and fell back to a comfortable second in command. Her getting popped though, changed everything. From that day forward, he had to take the reins and run shit the way he was born to. It had been a crazy three years, but the crew had made a name for themselves.

Word was traveling, that these youngins were the next up & comers and not to be fucked wit. "Well try not to stress so hard. You know rushing just leads to a whole bunch of mistakes. Have patience, and everything will work out." She encouraged. "Don't I know it, and thanks. That's why I love you."

He slid over and started kissing her neck. "Aight now, don't start nothing you can't finish boi." He slid his hands up her T-shirt and started caressing her already erect nipples. "This all man right here woman, and I got plenty of time to knock the linen outta that pussy."

She giggled as he lifted her shirt over her head then planted kisses down to her supple breasts. After showing them both equal attention, he lifted her up on the counter and slid her panties down her smooth, milk chocolatey, legs. He licked his way up from the arch of her feet. Her juices were already flowing, and when his tongue got to her moist box, he slurped up all her nectar. She threw her head back as his tongue went to work on her, and he showed her just how much he loved her.

6

Across town Baby G had a head of her own between her legs, that she was riding into her third orgasm. "Mmmm, mmhhmm, oo-ye-ye-yeeeeessss!!! Atleast I know one thing I'm gonna miss about this place." She let out as she creamed all around the lips attached to her. His tongue greedily accepted and searched for every drop it could find.

She opened her eyes to see his hardness throbbing at attention. "Mmm, make that two things." She paused provocatively then leaned forward and wrapped her lips around the tip of it. She gently caressed his balls in her hand as she slurped up and down his shaft making all 9' disappear, then reappear again. Simultaneously she went grinding on his face, her plump ass and fat lower lips damn near engulfing it. He could barely breath without turning his head the right way every now and then, but that only enticed him further.

He grabbed two handfuls of ass and dove deeper. 45 minutes later they were both spun, breathing hard, and dripping sweat. "Damn it's gon be hard to find somebody who can top that." She slid off of him and began putting on her state issued juvie uniform. "You betta stop playin with me before I put your ass on lockdown in here for your last six hours. If my phone ain't got your sexy voice coming through it by the end of the week, I'm a hunt you down then remind you why you shoulda used it... wit yo fine as."

He slapped her cheeks for emphasis and watched them ripple effect back to him. Then got up and started putting his own uniform on. They were in what looked like a solitary holding cell. It was the very same one they had been using for years. "Is that a threat Mr. Bossman, or a promise?" She eyed him seductively bending in front of him and looking back. "Aight, you keep on gurl and I'ma have to strap you down for old times sake."

She didn't know how he did it, or where it came from, but one day one of those insane asylum beds with the straps had appeared in there. She smiled as the memories of them taking turns back and forward on it, flashed through her mind. Fighting that familiar tingling sensation rising in her, she responded "Tempting baby, but the girls got something planned for me. You already kidnapped me long enough, they probably think a bitch snuck out on them. Just pull the same magic trick, make it appear in yo crib, and we can keep the good times rollin in the world."

He laughed as he lifted her up and they embraced one last time before leaving the room and having to jump back in character. When she got back up to population, he shoved her roughly through the door for effect before closing it behind her. She tried her hardest not to smile and look back. "Awww shit, there she go. Little miss trouble maker. For a second there, we thought a bitch was just gon leave without saying goodbye!" she cut her eyes at the luscious almond colored girl dramatically, then flipped her hair. "Bitch please, you know me better than that Jamisha, I just had to raise some hell one last time, and remind these hoe ass laws who really been running shit."

The group of girls in front of her laughed, while a couple "Mhm's & I know that's rights" rose up in response. "Yeah whatever, girl if you don't get yo ass over here so I can do something about that dead possum on yo head. We can't have you steppin back out in the world lookin like you done crawled up out a bando or something." That was her girl Trinity, dark chocolate skin, a little on the plus side, but carried it well on her 5'11 frame. Her hair was always on fleek and she made sure everybody she rolled with's was the same. She had 4 baby girls young as hell, so had the practice to run the salon when she got out.

As she plopped down on the floor in between Trinity's legs, the rest of the girls fell in to their normal routines. "Damn girl I still can't believe you leaving us. I still remember when yo stankin ass walked up in here. Everybody was whisperin like you was Cleopatra or some shit." MJ said as her long slender frame, with her puffed out natural afro almost made her look like a walking talking blunt. "Then big mouth Beatrice tried to start yelling out, "I don't give a fuck who da lil bitch daddy is, she can get it too just like the rest of these hoes." Thinkin she was hot shit."

A smile crept on their faces remembering what came next. Baby G constructed an innocent smile on her face and timidly walked up to where Beatrice was standing, who was now facing her defensively ready for something to pop off. Instead Baby G kept the young innocent girl act up and said, "You know, my daddy always told me that the loudest person in the room was the weakest. Now I usually don't waste my time wit weak ass bitches, but..." Suddenly all the innocence vanished from her face and was replaced with steel deadliness, "I don't take kindly to people disrespecting my daddy."

Before the light bulb in her head could hint her to the intentions of the girl in the front of her, a fist had already connected with her jaw. Baby G immediately followed up with a combination lookin like Tatiana Ali. Beatrice reeled back,

maintaining her balance until the unexpected right upper cut

brought the floor speeding towards her. Baby G immediately

pounced on her, "I'm sooo sick of you dis-respectful bitches,

talkin out the side of ya necks like ya'll bout something, but ain't

got ya-selves shit! What was that you was sayin now huh? I

could get it like the rest of these hoes right?! Is THIS how the rest

of these hoes been getting it huh? Huh bitch!? I don't hear you

talkin shit now bitch..."

Baby G was fuming while she relentlessly smashed the

girls head into the ground over and over with each sentence. It

all happened so fast nobody had time to react. That is, until De-

lani made her decisions and snatched Baby G off her, and carried

her to another section of the institution. At first Baby G's re-

action was to turn her rage on the owner of the strong arms that

grabbed her.

"I thought I was gonna have to choke your crazy ass out for

a second, but you proved that your instincts were pretty good after looking at me." She said leaning against the wall as she recanted the events. "Yeah well I guess real really does recognize real. Somehow I just knew you was friendly." The toned, almost muscular chick turned out to be her best friend as the days rolled.

As chance had it, her pops used to run wit hers back in the day, He would always sit and tell Delani stories of loyalty and legends & the shit they got into. One person he always spoke highly of was J Bug, said the man had saved his life on more than one occasion. Thus, the reason she chose to intervene on Baby G's altercation.

Baby G scrunched up her face, "I still don't understand why you saved that bitch, I'm sure I coulda got all 32 of those busted ass teeth up out of her mouth for her." Denali smirked, "Now I done already told told yo aggravated ass I wasn't saving her, it was you I was saving. If I didn't step in then, you damn sho wouldn't be walkin out them doors now."

She nodded her head in agreement, "sho you right about that, and that's why I love you. Shit that's why I love all ya'll thirsty ass bitches. We done had each other's backs through some thick and thin shit, no questions asked. Don't think this shit ends here, just because a bitch got her freedom. Each one of ya'lls days coming too, and we gon look out for eachother out there the same way we did in here. No bullshit."

They all sat silently for a while resonating on those words as they passed the joints around, until laughter unexpectedly erupted from somewhere in the group. Everyone turned to stare at Kandi's 5'5 red boned ass as she was bent over holding her sides. She looked like a video vixen goddess, having meat in all the right places, and washboard stomach. Her green eyes made an appearance, saw everyone staring at her, and just started rolling harder.

"Aw hell naw, that bitch geekin, no more weed for her she cut off." Stated MJ tryin not to crack up herself as a high reaction. "Um, you mind sharing with the class what's so damn amusing lil missy?" Trinity followed. After a few more seconds of trying to gather herself, she finally responded, "I'm still tryna figure out how this crazy bitch made that trick Crystal disappear into thin air."

Now filled in on the joke, it was everyone else's turn to crack up. "Bitch you ain't never lied. We damn sure ain't got no freedom or places to bury bodies. Yet this bitch makes a whole woman disappear on some Chris Angel shit." The laughter rises. "I told ya'll she got her walkin papers." To hell... she thought. "Mmhhmm, yea just up out of nowhere huh? I bet her papers ain't look nothin like yours."

Another fit of giggles struck. MJ done brought out that fire shit for the sendoff. Baby G thought feeling good as hell. "Yeah, and less than 24 hours after she threatened your life too." Chimed in Jamisha. "All coincidental and circumstantial ladies." She brushed off, only making them laugh harder.

It was true, that bitch Crystal had stepped out of line

talkin bout she had her fingers deep in the system, so just as the girls said, she made the bitch disappear. Sad that it was all over a petty place in line for a phone, and now she in line for the pearly gates. "Look at that bitch face, it look like she bustin a nut relivin it all right now." Kandi's voice snapped her out of her thoughts catching her dead to rights. She couldn't help but laugh her ass off with the rest of em.

Suddenly everything started hitting home at once. She looked around at her girls, and felt a pang in her heart. It definitely hadn't been a walk in the park the past few years, but her girls had made it a little less hell. She had come to this foreign place of modern-day child slavery, and found a new family, & here she was now about to be separated from them.

Her only comfort was knowing that this wasn't the end, and they'd all be meeting up on the other side to reign hell on the world. Her mood switch must've been contagious, because a sudden hush fell over the group as they all retracted into their thoughts. Her eyes landed on Kandi, and she had a flash of the previous night.

They had said their special goodbyes in private, and her pussy tingled thinking of the flavor of her juices running into her mouth as they devoured each other in a 69. She always loved the sweet mix of peaches and honey that her body seemed to naturally produce. Her lips so fat that when she put hers on them, they seemed to lock on and kiss back. They had been messing around on and off a couple years now, and it never got old with her. They had used everything from broomsticks to hotdogs in saran wrap on each other, and I'm sure could find plenty more if given the time.

As if reading her thoughts, Kandi's green eyes turned and locked onto hers, and winked. She could almost feel a jolt of electricity surge through the air. She was on the verge of creaming in her panties, when Trinity tapped her on the hand with the comb letting her know she was done. "Now that's the best doo I've ever done yet, so you better take care of it. I want a picture in

2 weeks and yo shit better still be bolted tight." She stated only half joking. Baby G thanked her both for the doo, and quietly for saving her from having to explain the puddle on the ground Kandi almost made her create.

They spent the rest of the day joking & reminiscing, a little crying, and making sure all contact info was exchanged. Before they knew it, time had flown by and they were all thoroughly baked when her name was called out. After some more tears, hugs, and a deep delicious kiss from Kandi, she was out processing and finally leaving the walls of a place she never wanted to see again.

7

Skiddlez sat in the back of the black – on – black stretch hummer, behind the 5% tint running plays through his mind, when he saw a female walking out awkwardly. He was about to turn away, until something about the outfit she was wearing held his attention. He slid the Cartier shades down his nose, then focused in harder, "Get the fuck outta here. It can't be…" he hopped out the back, "Well I'll be damned, look at you. So, the princess leaves and comes back a queen." He says out loud, getting her attention.

For a split-second Baby G looked at him with confusion until a look of recognition finally dawned on her face, followed by a wide smile. She ran and jumped into his embrace squeezing each other as he lifted her off her feet, "Skiddlez!!! Damn nigga, look at you." They finally separated, then stepped back and stood for a second taking each other in.

They both seemed to have hit growth spurts in the last few years. Only having the clothes, she was locked up in, her now 5'6 frame squeezed into the fabrics barely concealing the ass & titties that had grown wit her. "What the fuck they been feeding ya'll in there girl." He said as his eyes traveled appreciatingly up her body to her micro-braided hair. He had to blink a few times to make sure he wasn't trippin about how thick she had become. She was always attractive, but her little stint seemed to have turned her into a woman, and enhanced all the right places.

Likewise, her eyes were traveling over his broad muscular shoulders. "Whatever, let me find out you been out here taken them steroids." She countered. He sucked his teeth, "Mayne hell naw, this here's all natural. 12 Pack and all." He cockily lifted up his shirt to show off his ripped abs. Baby G had to fight the urge to reach out and run her hands across them.

Suddenly she became aware of what she was wearing, and how all her assets were all hanging out in front of him. An awkward moment passed between them as they stood staring at each other for a minute longer. Finally, Skiddlez broke the trance and shook it off, "Well shit, don't stand there lookin pretty, get yo ass in. You don't gotta wait for permission to do shit anymore, you're a free woman now."

She laughed and slid into the backseat, giving him a view he knew he'd never get from his mind. He shook his head and recollected himself before hoppin in after her. He knocked on the tinted partition to let the driver know he could go, before taking a seat opposite from her. A bucket of ice sat in the corner console with a bottle of Remy, Ciroc, Grey Goose, & Hennessey. A second bucket sat next to it with a bottle of Cristal & Dom Perignon in it. Next to that sat a cartoon of Newports, and a line of rolled blunts stuffed with the finest.

He waved his arms towards em like Vana White, "These are for you madam, take your choice." She laughed as her eyes scanned the array, "Damn boy, where's the party at? That's enough to get at least 20 people fucked up." He shrugged waving it off like it was nothing, "Shit you know WE do. As for the party, that's another story. Reach back there behind the seat and you'll find some more gifts to your liking."

She pulled the various bags of Fendi, Michael Kors, Louis V's, and more out. Prissy had all her sizes down pack, and set her up with everything from shoes to matching purses. Baby G almost shed a tear at the sight of it all. Without a second thought, she popped the tags off one of the fits she liked, then changed into it right there. It wasn't till after she looked up from admiring her new digs & how they fit, that she noticed Skiddlez nervously trying to turn his attention outside the window & giving her privacy.

She smiled inwardly, "My bad, guess I'm a little institutionalized. But look at you being a perfect gentleman." She teased. He shot her the bird and relaxed as she grabbed the bottle of Goose & poured up. She was still lit from the sticks wit her girls, but that didn't stop her from lightin up one of the pre-rolleds present.

They spent the rest of the ride catching up and getting lifted. He brought her up to date on all the business the crew was handling, and the latest events. Baby G soaked up everything she had been missing, and her mind already got to work on the future. By time she pulled up to her crib, they were thoroughly twisted. "Damn it feels good to be out bro, real shit. Thank you for real." She said with emotion lacing her voice. "Oh best believe, this shit ain't over. Just make sure yo ass is ready later, when I come back to scoop you."

She could barely conceal a smile as she looked at him, and shook her head. It was one thing for people to say they gon hold you down, and another to actually be held down. She heard of plenty people getting out and having not a damn thing, and to come out to this had her feeling the love for real. She gathered herself as she looked out at her crib.

The driver came around and opened the door for them, and they stepped out. She hugged Skiddlez hard, and they lingered there for a moment feeling each other's bodies pressed together. "Aight now girl, go on in there. Ya mama's been dying for her baby girl to come home. I'll bring these bags in for you, then catch up with you later."

She lingered for a second longer, caught up in the comfort of his arms before finally pulling away. (Girl get yo throwed ass in the house, before you molest this poor boy out here.) She thought, blaming the attraction on the drank and herb. She sobered up as much as she could, as she walked up the walkway.

Before she could touch the door, it flew open and her mother was squealing and wrapping her into her loving embrace. It took a second for her to realize she was squealing too, and they were both crying tears of joy like a couple of school girls on the front porch. Without realizing it, they had made their way into the living room talking a mile a minute and still arm in arm as if the other would disappear if they let go.

Skiddlez came down the steps, already having put all her things in her room. He gave mama a hug, a kiss on the cheek, and a wink. He hugged Baby G, then hollered, "Love ya'll both, catch ya later." And was out the door.

8

After taking a shower and scrubbing the filth of imprisonment from her body, she lay soaking in a bath laced with oils she hadn't felt nor smelt in years. Through this pampering, her mind drifted back to the conversation with her mother. After reconnecting and all the formalities were out of the way, her mother got serious with her and hit her with a dose of reality.

"...it's hard enough being black in America, on top of that a woman, without giving these people a reason to kill you or throw you in a cage like some animal. All that time in there, I bet you didn't pick up one book, or bother trying to learn the history of your people and the plight to get you all those opportunities you choose to take for granted?"

"Can you imagine what it was like to live in the 18th century as one of us? As soon as you boot up the new iPhone you got waiting for you in your room, why don't you google some people like Nat Turner & Freddie Douglas before you get to mindlessly wasting time on Facebook and Instagram? Throw in Sojourner Truth, and tell me which presidents helped the abolitionists when slavery seemed to be accepted as creed. You probably don't even know what an abolitionist is do you?"

She stared at her mother blankly and sheepishly, causing her to shake her head. Baby I know it's not easy to find yourself, and separate from the crowds & trends of everyone around you. Shit I was a wild child myself, until I had to grow up and get my mind right for myself and the people I love. Your father was so close to turning everything positive. He had so much vision, and is one of the smartest people I know. Everyone knows that hood legend, but I was blessed to know that good man inside who he kept guarded. If he could have achieved even half of what he had planned, he could have changed everything for the better that would have sent ripples across the world..."

"Instead, a person he trusted and probably would have given a kidney for, stabbed him in the back for pennies & peanuts. Now that same system he was about to change, enslaved him, and wrote him off as just another statistic. Out of all those people he kicked it with, cut for, and held down, I don't even need a full hand to count how many are there for him now. "

"Gabryiana Hays, you listen to me when I tell you... that is NOT what we want for you. We went through everything we did, so you would never have to go through the same trouble. The last thing your father wants, is for you to go following in his footsteps, and my heart couldn't take losing my baby girl to those same racist muthafuckas that took the only man I truly loved... Do you understand what I'm telling you baby? I need you to promise me that if there's anything you take from today, it's that you remember what I've just told you. Create your tomorrow, don't just live in theirs..."

Baby G had sat stunned and in tears by the words filled with so much emotion, that her mother had spoken. All she could do was promise, and hope she remembered to keep it. Even now as she lay in the tub, she felt the weight of those words.

They still hung with her as she got dressed to impress and headed downstairs to meet Skiddlez. Outside, the smell of the delicious feast her mother had stuffed her with, still lingered in the air as she made her way into the kitchen. To her surprise her mother sat at the table, as if she were waiting for her, with the remnants of tears in her eyes. "What's wrong mommy?"

Her mother wanted to tell her the feelings she was wrestling with. That she didn't want her to walk out that door. For them to just curl up on the couch and watch movies, and forget about the world like when she was her little angel... But she knew she wouldn't listen, and that the call of the streets was too strong. She could see it even now as her daughter stood in front of her, now an extremely beautiful young woman, with a look of worry in her eyes.

So against all her motherly instincts, she simply told her, "Just promise me you'll be safe out there please. Be the smart woman I know you to be, and trust your instincts no matter what. Remember what I said, and you make sure you bring yourself back home to me in one piece." Her mother's comments knocked her off her square, and she could detect something deeper lying beneath them. "Of course mommy, it's just gonna be a little welcome home celebration, then I'll be right back."

She kissed her on the cheek and hugged her tight. She hugged back like she was adamant to let go. When at last she did, Baby G stood for a second looking at her. She could feel a strong magnetic pull towards her mother, and began contemplating just staying home with her. When a knock at the door broke their trance. Skiddlez stood on the other side of it looking like a model out of the hood GQ magazine, rockin a matching blue monogramed Luis Vuitton Hoodie, pants, and belt set, sitting on top of some royal blue Luis Vuitton Jordan 4's fresh out the box.

He greeted them both with a hug and a kiss, and began escorting Baby G out when her mother grabbed him by the arm suddenly. "You make sure to watch her back tonight Thomas, and you bring my baby back to me safe & sound." Skiddlez looked up perplexed, but responded with a reassuring smile, "Of course mama, you know I wouldn't have it any other way. We just got her back, she ain't goin nowhere anytime soon if I have anything to do with it." He hugged mama tight, and gave her two pecks on the cheek and a wink, before turning away.

When they were in the car he turned and asked, "What was that all about?" Baby G shrugged her shoulders as she looked out the window at her mother who was still standing in the doorway. "I don't know," she waved one last time. "Probably just nerves from losing you for 3 years, you know how much your mama loves you. That's a damn good woman right there." He cranked up the whip and pulled off. The whole while saying goodbye, her mother's words from the day kept bouncing around in her head. Yet the further they pulled away, the further they fled along with the ominous feeling they carried. I guess it's true what they say, Out of sight, Out of mind.

9

After sparking the pre-rolled in the ash tray, Baby G's thoughts started drifting back to her girls in juvie. It was a little surreal to be free, after being incarcerated for all those years. It's unbelievable how much changes in so little time, when you're taken out of the game of life & put on the bench. When she was in there, there were plenty times where she thought she would never get out. Your mind gets to playing tricks on you, and you just accept that it's now your life. You block out as much as you can, and try not to think about what your missing so it doesn't hurt so much.

Then she thought of her father. He seemed to be locked up for an entire lifetime. What she had done was a mere second compared to him. Not to mention, he was serving actual time in a penitentiary. She couldn't even imagine what he was going through. Just that glimpse she had endured, made her heart cry out to him. She made a promise to herself to go and visit him the second she got a chance.

She tried to shake the thoughts before she became too emotional. That's when her mind snapped to something, "Oh my god, you kept her!" she squealed, running her hands over the interior of the Chevy Caprice. He had made a few modifications and upgrades, but sho nuff it was the same one from back in high school looking better than ever. Skiddlez looked at her like she was crazy, and snatched the blunt from her hand.

"Yeah, you only been riding in my baby for the past 15-20 minutes, and you just now noticing?" He patted the dashboard, with a look of pain on his face. "It's ok girl, don't mind her, she been gone so long she forgot how to appreciate nice things." She punched him in the arm playfully, "Boi stop, you know I love this bitch like she was my own. I like what you did to her, she definitely sexier than ever."

He puffed his chest out wit pride and raised his chin up cheesin, "Yoouu Knnoooww, I did a lil sum'n sum'n. Raised her up a bit, put some swangaz on her, upgraded the infotainment and some mo ish. Plus, of course, I had to go in on the system." To prove his point he cranked her up and opened the windows up. Soon she was swiveling her hips to a Migos track, that was blaring out of the car loud & clear like they were giving the streets a live performance. The bass was vibrating so hard around her, that it was making her pussy wet.

A few tracks later, they turned onto a street and started setting off car alarms. Baby G stopped dancing, "Damn! What the hell's goin on round here?" She yelled over the music. Skiddlez just smiled and kept driving. The street was packed with cars, and there were people literally EVERYWHERE. Baby G went on alert, fixed herself in the mirror, then focused on her surroundings. He saw her demeanor change and started laughing (There's the Baby G I know) he thought.

Her eyes were scanning any and everything that moved.

Everybody seemed to be heading in one direction, centering around some large three-story house. There were cones blocking the long winding driveway, but as they approached em, two guys ran out and moved them out of their way. She shot a sideways glance at Skiddlez, who was trying to unsuccessfully hide his ear to ear smile.

As they rode up the driveway, people started cheering & throwing their hands in the air. At the end, a big banner hung across the house that read [Welcome Home Baby G!] Since most the people in squad & attending were underage, he decided against a club. So instead he found one of those giant MTV Crib style houses to rent out for a night.

She read the sign, and her mouth dropped open. She slowly turned and looked at all the people outside of the car, who were now standing still hooting and hollering at the parked vehicle. Then she slowly turned back to Skiddlez, "Are you fuckin serious right now my nig!? You did all this for me?" He shrugged, "Well technically Da Squad did this for you. You ain't think we forgot about you, did you?" Everything finally registered, she reached over huggin him & kissed him on the cheek, "You know I love you right." It was all she could do not to cry. This was way more than she would have ever expected, and emotions were over-whelming.

She took a second to gather herself, then with a smile matching his, she turned and said, "Alright, I'm ready come on. We got a party to attend, and it would be rude to keep the people waiting." She grabbed her purse and threw some shades on, even though it was night time. "And the boss bitch has returned." Skiddlez stated, and with that they both stepped out into the awaiting crowd.

From there, things turned up more than a few notches. There was a live DJ set up in the living room which was also converted into a dance floor along wit the dining room. The kitchen was a bar, there were drinks everywhere you looked from freezer to pantry. The backyard was damn near the size of a football field. Three grills were going, there were two giant trampolines, and a boxing ring in dead center. Skiddlez & Ivory had arranged a cease fire for all attending local gangs, so anybody who had a dispute could handle it in the ring and leave it in the ring for the night.

That didn't stop the verbal shots though, "Who let the Dawgs out? Slobs slobberin on everything!", "Ya'll smell seawater? Then where the fuck all these crabs comin from?" It was all done in good nature though... For the moment. A pool and jacuzzi were present as well, and there were picnic tables littering nearly half the backyard.

The second floor had a pool table, tables set up where people were playing Bones & Spades. One room contained eight big screen plasma TVs with Playstations & Xboxes hooked up, while Madden and 2K tournaments were in progress. Money was spread everywhere from bets an everything. The room next door had Dance revolution, Just Dance, and some other games for entertainment. A couple girls were locked in team battles when she walked by.

Another room was set up as a movie theater, where people were doing things not so easy to get away with in a regular theater. On the third floor was the smokin room, the Champagne Room, and the squad's VIP room. The smokin room was full of bongs, blunt wraps, and papers. Baby G spotted something she didn't recognize, she was told it was a rig, which led to her getting her first taste of wax.

She floated from there to the champagne room, where there were two stripper poles set up and a TV playing music videos. There were actually strippers on the poles and niggas gathered around throwing money. One nigga even had a damn money gun, which he turned on Baby G when she stepped in. She couldn't resist doing a dance of her own as the money rained around her.

Everywhere she went people were handing her blunts

and drinks, coming up to hug or dap her up, & show their respect. Allot of people didn't know her, but knew of her or her father, and most of all that she was the reason this live ass party was being thrown. Finally, she made it to the last room in the house, their VIP room. It was technically the master suite and it was the biggest room in the house. Inside the squad lay in waiting loaded with their own entertainment & commodities.

The first thing she noticed upon entering the room was the 6'1 310 pds of bulging muscle mass that was now Ivory. Roscoe & Ant were engaged in a match of Call of Duty on a wall sized flat screen w/headsets on. Roscoe had a lit cigarette in his hand, and the ash was about as long as his finger but yet somehow still hanging on. Trackz was huddled over a laptop, his fingers moving at rapid speed beating down on the keyboard.

Jo-Jo and D-Money were posted up on the other side of the large room, on the barstools at the built in bar connected to the mini-kitchen, engaged in conversation with their eyes glued to their phones. Opposite that corner was a nice sized jacuzzi, where Prissy, Gina, and a female Baby G had never seen before, were soaking in their bikinis with Mui Tais in their hands. Ivory, always on point, saw them as soon as they entered playing security. His serious face instantly softened, and showcased his 32 white teeth at the sight of Baby G.

"Damn nigga, the fuck they been feedin yo ass, baby hippos, hormone steaks, and experimental drugs? Look at you Ivory, you look like some ancient African Demigod or something." Everyone in the room stopped what they were doing and turned their attention to the familiar voice. A high-pitched screech filled the room as Prissy damn near tucked and rolled out of the jacuzzi, then slip & slid across the room towards her.

Ignoring the fact that she was soaking wet, Baby G responded with her own squeal as they embraced and spun circles spinning a mile a minute. "Beesh look at you!" "Beesh I missed you so much!" "Beesh don't ever fuckin leave me again!" "Oh shit, Beesh got some ass finally." "Fuck you Beesh, you went and got more. And who did them cute ass micros?!" It went on like that for a minute.

Then everyone else joined in and had their turn. "Would you look at that, the princess done returned as a fuckin queen. Juvie done did you right." Roscoes said as his eyes traveled her body. "You betta watch it boi, before you get what you askin for. Three years is a long time, I might break ya." She joked. "And, I might like it." He joked back.

Ivory damn near made her disappear when he scooped her up and hugged her. Skiddlez brought Tasha over and introduced her, and they hit it off right off the bat. After all the tears dried, and hugs and kisses were out the way, D-Money cut in. "Now that the guest of honor has finally arrived, we can turn this muthafucka up for real!" He went in the humongous walk-in closet, that was the size of a normal bedroom, then returned with a black gym bag.

Five minutes later the long coffee table centered in the

sofas and love seats, was covered with an array of drugs from molly to shrooms. "Alright everybody, choose your poison, and enjoy the ride!!!" Lines of coke were cut up and evenly distributed. Drinks were mixed, and passed around laced with molly. Blunts were rolled, lit, and passed. Conversation was rolling, and the family was back in full effect.

A balcony was attached to the room overlooking the backyard, so a few of them stepped out to witness everyone doin they thang. Seeing them step out seemed to have a euphoric effect on everyone, as if witnessing royalty stepping out. The mass buzzed, swarmed, and yelled up to them. A dance battle started in the boxing ring. There were speakers all through the house linked to the DJ, his music, and microphones. So everyone was jamming the same thing no matter where on the property they were.

"Watch this, I've always wanted to do this since watching that movie Project X." Skiddlez said, retreating into the room. He returned with a back-pack and a microphone. Putting the microphone to his lips, his voice boomed through the speakers,

"Ya'll ever seen it rain Skittles before? Well get ready to taste the

rainbow!" With that, he removed giant Ziploc bags full of XOs

and started throwing them out over the crowd.

10

Once everyone realized what they were, it was a frenzy. Trackz had his phone out recording while the squad sat back laughing their asses off. "Aight folks, I think that it's about time we go and start mingling with the people. Can't let them have all the fun in this big palace." Ant yelled.

From there the night went from wild to insane. All the drugs started kicking in, and everything began to blur together. "Aww shit people, the queen has come to grace us with her presence on the dance floor. Welcome home Baby G! Ya'll know what time it is! If ya tired, then take ya weak asses home, because this is team No Sleep tonight and we just getting started." The DJ yelled over the speakers.

One minute she was on the dance floor breakin off whoever thought they were up to the challenge. Next thing she knew, she was in the smoke room taking another wax hit. Then she was in the backyard surrounded by some girls she remembered from school. Suddenly she was in the kitchen with a bottle in her hand. At one point she swore she saw a familiar face just standing in the crowd staring at her. She was surrounded by familiar faces, but something was off about this one. Besides the fact that everyone and everything was moving, this person was standing awkwardly still with intense focus on her... but her instincts were screaming at her that something was wrong with him.

She turned to see if anyone else noticed him, but by time she turned back he was gone. She was feeling so good, that she blamed it on the drugs and pushed it out of her mind. Shots of liquor went up, & blunts burned down. People were now skinny dipping in the pool and jacuzzi. The theater was a freak fest with nobody focused on the movie.

Somewhere in the mix she remembered bumping into a tall handsome light skinned guy with braids and tattoos. She shoved him into a nearby restroom and gave him the ride of his life. He tried to speak, and she shoved her tongue down his throat. She was feeling way too good, and she didn't want him to say anything to fuck up the vibe. His hard membrane was hitting all the right places, and she made no attempt to keep it down as she moaned and screamed what she wanted him to do next.

She bent over, showing him her voluptuous ass with her dripping peach smiling at him, and he wasted no time sliding up in her and going to work. She threw it back at him so hard he had to brace himself with the wall. With every stroke she got wetter and wetter as he went deeper and deeper inside her. Her eyes rolled in the back of her head as she felt her nut building up. At the same time, she could feel him begin to throb and knew he was about to bust. She pulled up all the way to the top of his dick and threw it all the way down to the base of his thick wet shaft.

Once, then twice, and the third time did it for the both of them as they came so hard they collapsed against the tub.

After a few minutes of lying there and not speaking, letting the waves of intensity course through her. She turned around and shoved her tongue down his throat one more time. Then she got herself together, stood, and left him there lying on the floor with a "Thanks sexy." Then she was swallowed up by the party again.

Back to the dancefloor, then watching some guys do keg stands as she smoked a blunt with a guy she used to know. Prissy found her, and told her Da Squad was heading to VIP for a recharge. Back in the room, everyone was breathing hard and sweating. "Yo, it is fuckin crazy out there!" Jo-Jo yelled overexcited and eyes wide. "I know right, this shit is lit. It's like the house is a living thing!" Trackz said with a look that matched Jo-Jo's. They each looked at each other and burst out laughing.

"Aight, round two!" Tasha yelled as she chopped the next

set of lines, and everyone gathered around the table. "Alright ya'll, this time when we go out there try and stay together. I wanna party wit ya'll more than anyone else." Skiddlez said. "True talk, I turned around and couldn't find anybody. I don't know where the fuck ya'll disappeared to." Roscoe added, "Shit, I don't even know where I went to half the time." Baby G confessed, and they all started laughing. "Ain't that the truth." Prissy hollered in between laughs, and everyone agreed. "At one point, I turned towards the camera and said, "The house has em now."" Trackz revealed. That was all they could take, half of em fell over laughing grabbing their sides. Even Ivory had a tear in his eye.

When they finally pulled themselves together, Tasha prepared them some molly laced shots. "To Baby G, welcome home Beeesh!" Prissy cheered, and they toasted then downed them. "I just wanna say, I love ya'll more than you'll ever know. Thank you for this, no bullshit. This is the best day of my life, 24 hours ago, I would have never imagined anything even close. There were days I didn't even think I was gonna make it, and felt like I was all alone in the world. Then to know ya'll been holding it down like this, and come out to this... That shits love ya'll, for real."

Baby G looked at each one of em seriously, "Awww bitch shut the fuck up before you get me cryin up in this muthafucka!" Prissy said hugging her. "We love you too Baby G, ain't nothin but a thang. You always held us down, and you kept it thorough through ya little bid, so it's only right." Skiddlez stated truthfully. "Yeah, real niggaz do real thangz." Ant said nodding his head. "And this the realest group of muthafuckas I know, True talk." Roscoe agreed, and everyone else nodded their heads in agreement.

There was a moment of silence, then Jo-Jo chimed in, "Aight that's enough of this drugged up Brady Bunch shit. Mo shots, mo molly, mo lines, mo caps, then let's get back to this party and enjoy this once in a lifetime experience!" Nuff said.

They did just that, and dove back into the party. This time they made double efforts to stay together, and keep within arm's reach of each other.

"Hol up, let's make a stop by the champagne room real quick." Roscoe cut in, "Last time I stepped in, it was lookin like a true-blue strip club. Maybe I'll buy everybody a table dance." He joked, but everyone followed as he led the way. When they stepped in, there was nobody on the poles, but there were plenty of private dances in effect.

In the far back, by some wall length mirrors, there was a small crowd gathered around. Men had their phones out, and were recording something the group couldn't see, so they got closer. "Eeewww, ya'll nasty up in heeerrr!" Tasha said with an amused smile on her face. In the middle of the circle were two butt naked girls, one's face was buried deep between the legs of the other girl. But that wasn't what made the girl's porn debut a spectacle.

The girl who was face down, ass up, was air tight, meaning all her holes were filled in the act of (DP) double penetration. Two men stood behind her with their pants around their ankles drilling their rods in and out of her snatch and ass simultaneously. Every now and then she would lift her head and moan, with a look of pure ecstasy on her face. The girl who was getting eatin out had a dick in her mouth, and one in each hand. She wore a crooked smile, and fixed a look of concentration on the shaft she was focused on. She seemed to work each one in sync, without losing the rhythm between her mouth and hands.

"Gaawd dayum, I knew something told me to come in here. These girls in here performin like they some certified pros." Roscoe said eyes wide. The group stood there mesmerized by the live flick in front of them for a while, with Trackz catching angles on his phone like he was the hired cameraman for the event displayed. Baby G couldn't lie, the shit was pretty hot, and she felt herself getting a little more than turned on by the grunts & moans accompanying the visuals.

It was the sound of skin slapping skin that was sucking them all deeper, but it was the sound of hand slapping head that snapped them back. "Damn nigga, close ya mouth, you actin like you wanna jump in there or something." Prissy hissed giving D-Money the side eyes. Gina snaked her head at Jo-Jo, "Yeah, ya'll wanna get next or something, let me find out." Jo-Jo & D-Money smirked at each other rubbing their heads, trying their hardest to hide their faces from their girls.

"Oh so ya'll think the shit funny huh, ya'll want a show huh? I'll give you something to look at. Watch a real bitch shit on these hoes wit some hood class." Prissy shot over her shoulders as she turned and walked off. As she was walking, she began shedding her clothes till she was down to nothing but her bathing suit. Then to everyones surprise, she jumped on one of the stages and started workin the pole and twerking the two slabs of ham she was workin wit.

Gina wasted no time in following suit and taking the other

side of the stage. Without a doubt, they were both ten times badder than the two girls in the back. Gina's half black, half Columbian genes gave her the perfect mix from her butterscotch skin to her firmly delicious coke bottle figure. Feeding off each other's energy, they both bent over and started making their asses clap. The sound alone was like the call of the Siren to the men in the room.

Once their eyes set on the four sets of cheeks gyrating on the stage, swallowing the strings of the swimsuit as if non-existent, a new crowd gathered. Baby G and Tasha started cheering them on, pulling out wads of cash and making it rain on their friends. Some guys started following suit, but the men in the squad quickly mad a barricade and kept them at a distance. Baby G, Tasha, D-Money, & Jo-Jo were the only ones stage-side. Both men smackin they girl's ass cheeks, and not to be outdone by the girls, throwing even more money on the stage.

After a while Baby G & Tasha decided to get up and join them, though they performed fully dressed. Men & women were hootin and hollarin at all the ass on stage workin it. Everyone knew who Da Squad was, so nobody tried to disrespect and push past the barricade. Instead they resorted to recording with their phones, to watch over and over again later. When they were done having their fun, they all jumped off the stage high-fiving and hugging eachother. When they got in the hallway, Skiddlez suddenly yelled, "Ya'll just gave me an idea."

They followed him as he swerved through the house. He didn't stop till they were in the living room, where he whispered something to the DJ, who in turn smiled and handed him a microphone. "OK everyone listen up, listen up. Ya'll know who it is, and for ya'll that don't, it's ya boi Skiddlez. I'm the reason that most these girls in here rollin hard and throwin the pussy so easily at you ugly ass niggaz." The crowd laughed, and some niggas good heartedly shot some random insults back.

"Anyways, Da Squad would like to give ya'll a little treat everyone has a chance to enjoy. In five minutes we gon have a twerk contest here on the dance floor, and all the females are invited to participate. The winner we gon toss a $500 prize to. So

ya'll come wit it, and men get ya phones ready."

11

If you asked anyone who was there, they would have sworn by it that the house literally began to shake. It was like a stampede as all the women in the house converged on the dance floor. Females in all shapes, sizes, and colors were coming out the woodworks. Soon there was a full blown twerk contest going down on the dance floor, and these girls were bringing their A-game.

One girl did a front flip into the splits, another walked up the stairs with no hands or feet... only her left cheek, then right cheek. Shit was wild, and the crowd was loving it. Skiddlez was on the mic hosting it all, adding a bunch of comedic effect with his "Oh my god, did you see that!" s & "Everybody better hold on to something, this girl's gonna cause a earthquake!" ad libbing.

Baby G was sitting there watching Skiddlez thinking about how much of a natural he was in the spotlight, when Tasha tapped her on the arm and said she had to go to the bathroom. Ant was the closest person nearby, so they got his attention to escort them. The closest one was by the kitchen, so they wouldn't have to go too far from the squad. On the way back, they stopped in the kitchen to get a drink. That's when Baby G got the feeling in her gut again.

As if in response, someone whispered in her ear. "Itzzz gooth tooth seeth youth again. I been waithin for youth to come bakth." By time she turned around, she could only see the back of a head walking off. Something about the voice was familiar, but she couldn't recall knowing anybody with an intense lisp that bad. It was almost like a snake was talking to her. For some reason a picture of the snake from the Jungle Book hypnotizing Mogley popped into her head.

"Who was that?" Tasha asked, shaking her from her thoughts. "Honestly I have no idea." She answered confused.

She tried to shake it off, but something kept nagging at her. No matter how hard she tried though, she couldn't seem to place that voice. As they were grabbing their drinks and turning to head back to the group, Tasha tapped her again. "Well he's over there just staring at you. What's the creep's problem?"

When she followed Tasha's gaze, she saw the very same face she had seen staring at her earlier in the night. Once they made eye contact he smiled, but the smile didn't reach his eyes. He opened his mouth and yelled across the crowd, "Oh soth youth don'th remeberth me nowth huh?!" Just as the words met her ears, Ant pulled up next to her and said, "The fuck is Henry's bitch ass doing here?"

At the mention of his name, the memories came floating back, of the bathroom a few years ago. Her eyes grew wide and her gut clenched as that bad feeling took over, that she had just got caught slipping. His smile grew wider in response as he yelled, "Heyth one seconth, my thriend Mack wanth to holler at youth!" The world moved in slow motion as his hand came up wit a Mac-10 squeezing.

Baby G could see the flashes from the barrel before the sound reached her ear. Bodies began dropping between them. Screams rose, and the house broke into mayhem. All the while, the muzzle was sweeping closer and closer towards her. Looking down the barrel, it seemed she was looking death in the face.

Then she felt her body knocked to the ground. After shaking the shock off, and realizing she was still alive, she opened her eyes to find Skiddlez laying on top of her and Tasha next to her. He had dove and tackled them both to the ground. The sound of gunfire and screaming filled the air as feet ran every which-a-way.

Looking around she saw a bunch of bodies on the ground, and off to her right there was a girl holding her stomach and crying. Looking closer she could see the blood pooling around her. She looked behind her and began to cry herself. On the floor with his eyes wide, and a bullet in his head lay Ant's now lifeless body. "Ant noooo!" She heard someone scream, then realized it was her.

She tried to get up and move to him, but found Skiddlez was still on top of her. She instantly feared the worse and started screaming his name, "No no no, Skiddlez get up! Skiddlez please!" She shook him, and her hand came away from his back coated in blood. Her screams grew more frantic as she tried to roll him over. "Tasha help me, I think he's hit! Skiddlez get up please!"

He started coughing, "I'm good, chill. I'm good." He finally rolled off her. He rolled his shoulder, and winced. "The muthafucka got me, but it was just my shoulder. I'm good." She hugged him tight, "Don't fuckin do that to me." Then she re-membered, and pointed at Ant. Skiddlez followed her finger, his face dropped as he saw Ant laying in his own blood.

"Fuck no, I'ma kill that muthafucka. You and Tasha

head for the back door and get out of here, I'll handle this muthafucka." At the mention of Tasha's name, they both turned to where she was laying at. "Tasha you hear me, you and Baby G get out of here. Now!" Skiddlez yelled grabbing her hand, he already had his .380 in his other ready to go.

Tasha looked at him, and tears started falling from the side of her eyes. Her mouth was moving, but there were no words coming out. She looked like a fish outta water. Realization dawned on Skiddlez, and his heart dropped along with his gun. "Tasha baby get up, come on. I'm sorry I didn't mean to yell at you, get up baby, please. You gotta get outta here." He wrapped his arms around her, to lift her up, and felt her laying in something wet.

He pulled one hand from underneath her to see it bloody. Now the tears began falling from his eyes. He lifted her shirt, and saw three bloody holes across her torso. "No baby, Noooooo! Get up. Come on baby, get up Tash. We gotta go home. I'll make you dinner. We got shit to do baby, get up. Don't do this to me please. Don't leave me please."

Skiddlez was breaking down as he cradled Tasha's body. Her lips kept moving, and he put his ear near her mouth to try and hear, "I... L-L-Looovve... you... T-T-Tommy..." He managed to make out after a few attempts. That was all he could take, "I love you too Tash. Don't worry, it's gonna be alright. I'm gonna get you to a doctor, it's okay baby, stay with me." But when he looked up, her eyes were staring off to the side, empty of life, and her lips had stopped moving.

Baby G sat to the side with tears streaming down her face witnessing everything. All the fight went out of Skiddlez as he collapsed on top of Tasha's body screaming and crying. While this was goin on, Henry, thinking he had gotten Baby G when she fell, had turned on the rest of the crowd. He was spraying around in a circle at anything that moved. His face was manic as he felt the power of the gun in his hands, and the bodies dropping all around him.

He had brought 5 extra clips, and was already on his 4th one. Bodies were piled everywhere, people were screaming and crying, and it all turned Henry on. He stuck his tongue out licking the air, revealing the serpent split that had been givin to him years ago. He'd been plotting his revenge for years, but never actually thought he'd be able to go through with it.

He definitely never thought it would feel this good. He actually had a hard on, and noted he was laughing and yelling now. After loading his 5th clip, he knew he had to start making moves for an exit. He took two steps toward the door, but couldn't help but turn back and lean on the trigger some more. Once that clip clicked empty, he reluctantly turned to exit through the front door.

The minute his body turned around, Ivory's Nina pressed against his temple and discharged without hesitation. Henry's body slumped to the ground with the manic look still frozen on his face, and a bulge in his pants. Now that the gunfire had ceased, all you could hear was cries of pain and terror. Ivory yelled out to Da Squad, "I got him, everybody good? Baby G, Skid-dlez, Roscoe, D-Money, everybody sound off!" One by one people began to come out of their hiding places.

Screams now turned from terror to anguish as others laid their eyes on their fallen family and friends. Jo-Jo & Gina appeared from behind the DJ booth. Roscoe came from behind some furniture yelling for Ant. Trackz slowy rose a few seconds later. D-Money and Prissy came down the steps with D-Money in the lead. "Over here!' Baby G stood, and the tone of her voice made them all come running.

Roscoe was the last one to make it, because he was running through the house looking for his brother. There were bodies everywhere. Some people were so high and fucked up, that they got shot forgetting they had their own weapons. Some people got trampled by others in the frenzy to escape. It's crazy how the human mind reacts in moments of life-threatening terror.

"Yo has anybody seen Ant, I can't find him nowhere." By

then everyone else had already seen, and one by one their heads dropped. "Why ya'll lookin like that..." He stated frantically, then he saw Skiddlez cradling Tasha with a distant look in his eyes while he rocked back and forward. He started towards them then stopped when he noticed some familiar Jumpman's layed on the floor.

His eyes traveled up the starched jeans, and bulged out when they landed on his brother's face. "Naw bro, naw mayne, not my brother. Please no..." he ran to his brother's lifeless body and let out a heart wrenching cry of anguish and loss. There was nothing anybody could do... Death had claimed it's victims, and there were no returns.

12

The month that followed was filled with funeral after funeral. 41 people had been killed, 23 injured, and everyone was traumatized. The news was calling it the House Party Massacre, and it was one of the biggest tragedies to hit young adults outside of school in the century. Kids were sometimes attending two to three funerals a day.

People of all nationality and class were affected. Everyone from the mayor's kids to the preacher's were in attendance. Fingers were being pointed everywhere. Of course Da Squad came under fire to take responsibility, but ultimately the blame landed on Henry's family.

Ant's funeral was tough, but there was a sense of togetherness as everyone supported. His parents knew how close all of them were, and harbored no ill feelings toward anyone in Da Squad. Instead they leaned on each other for support, and reached out to them for help to keep Roscoe from plummeting too far into depression.

Tasha's funeral was the exact opposite. Her parents blamed Skiddlez, and everyone connected to him, for their precious daughter's death. When they showed up, her mother immediately charged at Skiddlez and slapped him. He just stood there as she continued to beat on his chest in tears, and call him everything in the book. It stung hearing her say it was his fault, but he already blamed himself so he accepted it all. It was her father who finally collected her, and allowed them to attend on account of his daughter's love for him.

That night the squad gathered at Skiddlez, and used to be Tasha's, crib for their own vigil. Everyone was fucked up, but Roscoe & Skiddlez were inconsolable. Roscoe had adopted an alcohol problem, while Skiddlez was popping pills like crazy. Both were smoking like chimneys. Secretly Baby G had been feeling responsible for everything. In her mind, all this happened because she had come home.

"I still can't believe that lil snitch ass, bitch ass nigga Henry did all this." Jo-Jo said as he took a swig from his cup. "We underestimated him, we threatened and tortured him, then took our eyes off him and forgot him." Ivory responded, "Well never again, from now on we just straight bodying muthafuckas. I don't give a fuck if it's just over a dollar!" Roscoe fumed drunkly.

"I know you hurtin Roscoe, but we can't just go around bodying everybody for nothing." Prissy interjected rationally. "Da fuck we can't." He challenged. "She's right, we just gotta be allot smarter about how we handle shit. No more of that kid shit, underestimating muthafuckas." Trackz added.

Roscoe jumped up like he wanted to say something more, stared Trackz in the eyes, then huffed and slumped back down on the couch. He wanted to lash out, but he knew Da Squad was family. "Yo Skiddlez, you good my nigga?" D-Money asked concerned. Skiddlez didn't even bother to respond, he just kept staring at the wall that held a picture of him and Tasha. That's all he'd been doing the whole night. D-Money dropped his head, and puffed on the spliff he was holding.

Baby G walked over to where he was sitting, and gave him a comforting hug. She went to Roscoe and did the same, then finally, went and sat next to Skiddlez. She embraced him, but instead of letting go she just put her head on his shoulder. Allot of thoughts had been going through her mind, but there was one reoccurring one in particular. She figured this was the best time if any to voice it.

"There's something I wanted to talk to ya'll about." She started. Everybody's head turned towards her except Skiddlez's, who remained on the picture. "Now ya'll can't tell me I'm trippin, but I've thought this all the way through & can't get it off my mind... Now ya'll know that nigga Henry's funeral is next week, right?"

Roscoe rose back off the couch angrily, "Fuck dat bitch ass nigga Henry. If he was still alive, I'd fuckin kill him. Fuck him and everybody who fucks wit him." Baby G let him get it out, "That's actually my thoughts exactly," She continued, "That nigga took family from us... He took our friends, he took pieces of our hearts. His life isn't enough." She paused to let that sink in.

"So, what you tryna say?" JoJo asked. "I'm saying... He touched our family, so we touch his... and anybody who fuck wit him..." For the first time all night, Skiddlez took his eyes off the picture. He simply looked at her and smiled, and just like that it was on.

13

"We gather here today to mourn a tragic loss. A child who had his whole life ahead of him, for whatever reason, our father chose to bring home early. It's times like these we have to have faith and remember that He has a plan, and we must trust in that plan even when we don't understand it..." The preacher continued to talk to the crowd gathered in front of him, and surrounding the raised casket.

Many tears were being shed, but none came close to the boy's mother who had to be held up, in fear of collapsing, by her husband. A young girl in her early teens stood shocked, mostly from the loss of her brother, but also because of how many people showed up. They weren't the most liked family in the community at the moment, still the entire family from youngest to oldest had come together and made an appearance for support.

"At this moment, I would like everyone to bow their heads in prayer." Everyone's heads dropped, and eyes closed, leaving them oblivious to the tinted vehicles approaching. Five figures hopped out with ski masks & gloves on, and black from head to toe. Each branded an assault rifle with extendos, and extra clips on the hips.

As the preacher continued his prayer, the figures fanned out in a line. "When ya'll see Henry, give him this message for me. FUCK YOU!" one of them yelled, and with that they opened fire into the crowd. Before any of them could register what was happening, half the crowd had already been sprayed. Few tried to run, but the men methodically mowed down every one of em until no one was left standing.

Three figures turned back towards the vehicles, but one stepped forward and approached the strewn-out bodies. He raised his gun and proceeded to fire extra rounds into each one of the bodies. The other man quickly joined him. When the clips ran dry they each reloaded, then turned their fire on the coffin. As the bullets riddled and splintered the wood to pieces, the supports gave way and it dropped in the hole spilling the corpse out sideways.

Changing their target, they put the rest of the clips into the corpse. It seemed to dance in response, so hard that it's body parts separated from each other like a crash dummy upon impact. "From dust we came, and to dust we return... Rest in pieces pussy." Skiddlez spat. "Amen." Roscoe followed, making the cross with his two middle fingers. Then they ran back to the vehicles, and fled the scene.

Just like that, an entire bloodline had been wiped from the face of the earth. Since Henry had claimed so many victims, the list of retaliation included everybody in the city & then some. So the authorities had their hands full with the cases, which would most likely turn cold first. With allot of his victims being cop's kids, and children of politicians, not many could seem to find it in themselves to care. An eye for an eye, a massacre for a massacre.

Later that day, after disposing of the vehicles, clothes, and everything involved, the squad returned to Skiddlez's crib. Prissy and Gina let out collective sighs of relief when they saw everyone walk through the door in one piece. "Oh my god we were so worried, it's all over the news!" Gina exclaimed jumping into JoJo's arms. "Everything straight?" Prissy asked as D-Money approached and gave her a kiss.

He looked at Roscoe, who looked at Skiddlez... then a smile broke across their faces, "Yeah everything's gravy." Skiddlez confirmed. With that they started a mini-celebration. What they had done didn't erase or undo the pain caused by their losses, but knowing they did something for vengeance made them feel a little bit better inside. After the bottle was gone, and the blunts were burned, it was time for them to part ways.

"Aight everybody, remember the story and watch for them hataz on ya'll way to the cribs." Baby G ordered. Trackz had doctored an undetectable video with a time stamp on it, showing that they were all together mourning their friends during the time of the shooting. Just in case twelve showed up asking questions. Everybody embraced and said their goodbyes and good lucks in case the unexpected happened, then were off.

After closing and bolting the door, Baby G turned and went straight for the kitchen. She removed a fresh bottle of Bacardi, then poured two shots. Since the party she'd been staying over more & more, mostly to keep an eye on Skiddlez, but also because she enjoyed the freedom. She'd damn near converted his guest bedroom into her room.

Though he couldn't lie, he definitely wasn't against the comfort of the company. She walked over and handed him the shots, "To a successful mission." They clink glasses and downed them. He smiled & returned back to the swisher he was rollin as she poured more. "Damn nigga, I almost forgot what that looked like." He looked up at her quizzically, "What?" She grinned, "A smile on yo face boi. It looks good on you."

He rolled his eyes & mushed her playfully. "Fuck you... but you right. I guess revenge is sweet. I finally feel like I did something for my baby." His eyes inadvertently shot to the picture on the wall. She caught the look and tried to keep the mood upbeat. "I hear that, shit got a bitch's adrenaline sky high. Mowin all them pussy ass niggas relatives down, was like a high of all the best drugs rolled into one. Shit got my body tingling, and my pussy still ain't dried up. You lucky I ain't bailed on yo ass, and went to find me somebody to scratch this itch."

Skiddlez almost choked on the puff he had just inhaled. "Girl you'z a damn freak! Only you would get off on some shit like that." He joked, "But on some real shit, I feel you, dat shit got me amped up too. If we ain't had to lay low, I'd hit da city doin a buck fifty."

She smirked at him, "Oh, so I'm a freak. Yeah you got that,

but you can't tell me that shit ain't turn you on. I seen you, for a second there I didn't know what you was up to. Then when you rolled up on the coffin like that, the way you was standing I could tell you was on one. You my nigga and all, but I swear dat shit made a bitch sneak a nut."

Her hand slid down between her legs, and his eyes followed. When he looked up, she was looking at him, and their eyes locked. Everything in the universe seemed to stand still, yet like a magnet their faces drew closer. Before she knew what was happening, she found herself straddling him feeling his rock hardness, trying to bust out his pants, swelling beneath her.

When their lips touched, the world exploded. It was a feeling neither one of them had ever felt. It was as if they were under water trading the same air for survival. When they separated their tongues, and opened their eyes, they were both naked without remembering how they got that way. In one fluid motion, he lifted her and slowly lowered her on top of his stiffness and penetrated her lips. He filled up every inch of her like two perfect pieces, and she was so wet they both made their own noises of surprised ecstasy.

Their tongues reunited, and she began grinding her hips into him slowly at first, then faster and harder. His hands were cupped on each cheek guiding and adding extra force into each rotation. He reached one hand up and grabbed a fistful of hair and yanked her head back. As she released a moan, he took one of her bouncing breasts into his mouth and began thrusting into her.

The combined sensation brought on her first nut, and her juices coated his shaft dripping down both their legs. "Oh fuck Tommy, mmhhhmmm, right there." He pinned her back on the table and lifted her ankles over his shoulders and began digging deeper into her. "Damn this pussy feel so good that I wanna dive in the muthafucka!" and that's just what he tried to do, dick first.

He had his arms hooked under her shoulders as he pile-drived into her guts. Her eyes were rolling back into her head as she cried out his name and her toes curled. It wasn't long before she began to approach her second nut, "Ohhh sh-sh-shiiittt, I'm cu-mm-in agaaiinn!" She cried as she unloaded another stream and her body convulsed. The pressure of her nut against and around his dick only made the pussy feel that much better.

He pulled out and started slapping it against her clit. The sensation sent more waves through her. She regained control and used her feet to kick him to the floor, then dropped on him. Now having the control, she rode him like a stripper, making her ass clap as she bounced on top of him. She used her pussy muscles to grip him tighter inside her and milked him for every-thing she could. It was his turn for his eyes to roll in his head.

"Oh shit girl, you bout to make a nigga bust. God dayum that shit feel good." He said feeling his nut building up. His words brought her closer to hers, and she leaned over and dropped her lips down to his as she lifted to his tip and slid it down on his rod over and over, harder and harder, until they both erupted damn near swallowing each other. She continued riding him as their juices mixed, tryna squeeze out every drop of the nut while her body shook into him.

She collapsed on top of him, and lay there with his arms wrapped around her. Their heavy breathing was all that could be heard, as they both got lost in their thoughts. Now that his body got what it wanted, his mind began to take over, & he was overcome by mixed emotions. On one hand he felt guilty as if he'd just disrespected the memory of Tasha, on the other he'd never felt with anyone, anything like what he just felt with Baby G. That made him feel guiltier and hella confused.

Baby G was trying to sort out her own feelings. She had no idea what the fuck that was that just happened, but all she knew was that she wanted more of it. She could feel him getting distant already, and already figured what his thoughts were probably on. So she took control as usual, sliding her tongue into his mouth.

The air around them crackled and he could feel himself stirring. When she pulled away and locked eyes, he could read the need within them. Before he could say anything, she put her fingers to his lips, slid down his body, and took him into her mouth. Sho nuff she got what she wanted. They spent the rest of the night exploring each other in every way they never had.

14

In the morning she woke to a text from her mom: [Come home now, we need to talk]. "Shit." Was all she could say. She figured the laws must have shown up to the crib or something. After getting Skiddlez up & getting ready, she thought of what she was gon say the whole ride over. When he dropped her off in front of her house, she was so lost in her thoughts that she payed no mind to the fact that they hadn't said one word the whole ride, or the awkward goodbye that just occurred.

She walked the path up to her house in slow motion, as if she were walking the Green Mile to the chair. Walking in the house, the first thing she noticed were the bags packed by the door. The second, were her mother's eyes as she sat on the couch, that were stained red as if she'd been crying the whole night. "Sit." Were the steel cold words that escaped her lips as she saw her daughter enter.

"So juvie was fun was it? Who'da thunk you enjoyed being a chained up slave, & caged like an animal..." Baby G's face scrunched up, "No mama I..." Her mother continued as if there were no one else speaking, "You've been out of the system's hands for a couple months, and already your begging them to take you back. Your father sacrificed his life & his freedom so you wouldn't just be some welfare baby raised in the projects, subjected to the horrors we had been.

I've worked myself to the bone to make sure you never wanted for a single thing, not a day under this roof have you known hunger. Women have come a long way in society, & the blood and sweat of black people that have fought with their every being, paved the way for your freedom, opportunities, & rights today. Yet with all these options, that no black woman before you could have even imagined, you choose to willingly sign yourself up for slavery & oppression."

The weight of her mother's words started weighing on her, "That's not what I..." A swift finger raised, cut her words off, "Maybe I was foolish. Since a little girl, I pictured you going to college. Your just so damn smart... Then I saw you as one of those successful women wearing a business suit to work, married, giving me like 10 beautiful grand babies, and making your husband stay home to watch them." A brief smile crossed her face, then disappeared.

A picture of Skiddlez flashed in Baby G's mind just as fast. "Instead I get the same results as if I would have picked up the glass dick, or been walking the streets sellin my pussy to every weak ass nigga wit a buck. Or maybe I shoulda just followed your father into prison, and left you out here parentless. Maybe then, you would have fought to make something out of yourself instead of... Look... I know it's hard losing your friends the way you did, but what ya'll did to that boy's family was just evil.

Don't you dare sit there and try to deny it to my face neither and insult my intelligence, because then you'll make me have to put my hands on you and I'm trying my best to have a civil conversation... I'da been surprised, if you weren't your father's daughter, but I've seen and been a part of worse. Still, I can guarantee you this is the last thing your father wanted for you. We DID NOT risk everything, for you to just throw your life away... Grab my purse right there, and reach inside."

She did what she was told, & was shocked at what her hand brushed over. She looked at her mother with an uncertainty, "Go head, pull it out. I know it ain't no foreign feeling to you." Baby G's eyes grew wide as she removed the pistol from her mother's purse. "Mama, why do you have a gun in your purse?" Without warning, her mother grabbed her hand and placed the barrel of the pistol to her heart.

"Pull the trigger." She said with her eyes boring into her. "Go ahead, pull the trigger!" Tears streamed down Baby G's face, "Noooo, mama. Nooo, I can't, I don't want to. Please, what are you doing?" Her mother's cold expression didn't change as she held the gun in place. "If you're going to continue to go out in them streets, and act the way you've been acting, throwing your life away... Then pull the trigger now, because either way you'll be killing me. Except that way, you'll be doing it allot slower and more painfully. So, if those are your intentions, then I would rather you put me out of my misery now. Your all I've got left, and I'd rather lose my life to you now, then to lose you to these streets later."

Baby G's hands shook violently as she cried uncontrollably. The truth in her mother's words were too much for her to take in. Shame, confusion, and a number of other emotions, were racking her body in waves. "Mommy please... I'm sorry... Please, I can't... I don't want too. I'm so sorry." Her mother finally released her hand, allowing the gun to drop to her side. Baby G immediately threw it on the couch.

Her mother cupped her face in her hands, and forced her to look her in the eyes. "Then promise me... promise me you'll at least try to do better. Promise me you'll makes something out of yourself, and do something meaningful with your life. Promise me, and remember that your word is one of the most important things you carry in this world."

She looked her mother in the eyes, seeing all the hurt and pain within. She thought about her words, and made a life changing decision right there. "I promise mama, I'm sorry. I didn't mean to hurt you so much. I wasn't thinking about anybody but myself... I'm sorry for putting you through so much mama. I promise I'll do better." Her mother studied her eyes for a moment, then satisfied with what she saw there, she released her face and pulled her in for a hug.

Baby G immediately collapsed into her mother's embrace as if she were a little child again, seeking all the comfort & love she ever had. "Remember your promises, and always keep your word." Baby G nodded her head against her mother's chest, "I will." A knock on the door imposed on their intimate moment. "That's for you."

She looked at the door, then at her mother trying to comprehend those words through all she was feeling. "I'm sending you to live with your aunt & uncle for a while. You've made too much noise out there in the streets. You'll be lucky if the police don't come looking for you. Still, there's things you don't understand about this world and your actions. Even when you think you've gotten away with something, the world's still gonna make you pay. There's always something you didn't factor coming into play. Whether it's a scorned lover, a vengeful friend, or just plain karma. When you take a life, especially as many as ya'll have, somebody or something is out there to serve you vengeance & justice. I have to do everything I can as a mother to prevent that. I can only pray that's enough. If you keep your promise, then just maybe you can offset things & make it all right again."

Baby G just stood there stunned as she took in everything. She both understood, and didn't at the same time, and responded with inaction. "Come now, give me my love to hold me over in your absence, then get your bags over there, and go with your uncle. Most importantly, remember your promise."

No longer tethered to this world, she did just as her mother told her. Floating in a dream-like state, she tatted everything that had happened since she walked through the door, to her memory and soul. Her heart and mind were still in the house, even as her body drove away in her uncle's car toward the unknown.

15

[Several months later.] "Aight, it's game time. Everybody knows what to do, let's get in and get ghost. Trackz, what we lookin like?" There was a brief silence before the response came through everyone's earpiece. "They've been officially hacked & blocked out. Their cameras are now our cameras, boss." Trackz confirmed from his computer base, disguised as a delivery truck, parked not far away.

"What I tell you about that boss shit?" Skiddlez replied immediately. "Sorry boss." Was the come back, and you could hear a single chuckle from the rest of the group. "Fuck all ya'll. Aight get serious. Our opening should be here in a couple minutes. Ya'll know the motto." He stated seriously. "Everybody dies, no excuse flies!" Everyone joined in on the squad motto.

They all stood decked out all black from head to toe, in some military ninja gear their employer had gifted them after their last job. Every inch of their skin was covered, their masks even had some mesh type material over the eye and mouth areas. This made it so you couldn't but guess what race they really were, and it was a no-go spotting any identifying details. Not that they ever left a witness to take a statement anyways.

"Mayne these suits it's too cold, got a nigga feeling like a cobra commander or some shit." Jo-Jo said lowly. Though no-one responded, they all had to agree. Then right on cue the back door flew open, and a man came out holding two large garbage bags. Just as he tossed the second bag in the large dumpster, two holes appeared in his back from Roscoe's silenced nine milie, and Ivory effortlessly tossed the body in with the rest of the trash.

D-Money held the door open as everyone filed in. Wordlessly they all separated onto their set paths they'd gone over a hundred times through recon. The strip club that was usually jumpin stood empty except for a few employees, and some straggler strippers that had nowhere else to be. The squad had planned it like this, for a few hours each week the club closed to clean, inventory, and count money.

The music played for the empty club without a DJ, adding extra cover for the squad. They slid through the dimmed setting, sticking to the shadows towards their destination. D-Money & Jo-Jo flanked the top floor, while Roscoe covered the opposite side, of the bottom floor, from Skiddlez who had Ivory trailing close behind. Ivory deemed himself Skiddlez's personal protector, and never allowed him far out of his sight on a mission.

D-Money made first contact, catching one of the security off guard as he stood a few feet from the balcony overlooking the club. *Phew... Phew* came from his silenced weapon, and he caught the body before it could tumble over. Then he sat him in the nearest couch as if he were just chillin. "One down." He confirmed over the com.

Roscoe came up on the V.I.P. area, and quietly slid in to check each room. He stopped when he came to the last one, hearing sounds on the other side. Pistol ready, he crept into the room undetected by a stripper with a Cardi B's ass up in the air while doming up one of the employees. The man's head was dropped back with his eyes closed, showing that lil mama was working with something.

Roscoe sent a bullet through the man's jaw, and straight to the brain. Then he leaned back on the wall amused, watching the stripper literally suck the man's soul out of his body for another 30 seconds. "I gotta know... is his dick still hard, or is it so small that you can't tell the difference? Bitch you been suckin a dead man's dick for the past minute."

Startled the stripper slowly turned to the voice as the words sunk in. Seeing nothing at first, she glanced back at her secret lover noticing the hole in his head. Before she could scream, a hole appeared in the side of hers, silencing her forever. "One guard, one dead stripper to match." He communicated to the others. From what they knew, there should be fifteen people hiding in the building. That left twelve more.

Ivory & Skiddlez came up on the two sitting at the bar with a bottle between them. Ivory raised his gun, but Skiddlez halted it's upward progress shaking his head no. "Watch this, there's something I always wanted to do." Ivory shrugged, and sat back as Skiddlez crept around to the side of the bar. He lined them up perfectly in his sights, and fired one round that went through them both simultaneously.

"Fuck a game, now that's some real-life COD shit nigga!" He whispered excitedly, scratching the act off his bucket list. Ivory smiled in response, "Fuck two girls one cup, I'll watch two niggas one bullet any day." They dapped each other up, then instantly got serious and back to business. "Two more down." He confirmed to Da Squad.

Da Squad covered the rest of the building eliminating targets till they all met up by the last door. By their count, there were only three left, and one of em was the target. They were also the most trained and armed, so they had to be extra cautious getting into the fortified room. If they were lucky, they'd catch them off guard, but they weren't about to bet their lives on it.

Ivory had been carrying a riot shotgun for the occasion, and was just about to bust the door off the hinges, when Trackz's voice came over the com. "Uh guys, you got company coming through the front door. If I'm not mistaken, I think it's the target's baby mama." Everyone's head turned to the front of the club, just as outside light shined in from the opening door. "Nobody shoot, I got a plan." Skiddlez commanded.

They all faded back into the shadows, as the woman walked through the club oblivious to the dead bodies it held. It was obvious she was a dancer from the way she moved, even stopping to twerk to the song playing over the speakers. "Good laaawwd, that bitch look like Buffy Da Bodie. Please can I keep her?" Roscoe's voice came over the com.

"You know the rules my nigga." Came the response. "Maan, you never let me have nothing Dad." He joked back. "Ssshhh, before I take away your video games for a month." Everyone tried their hardest to stifle laughs as the bitch approached the targets door. She rapped on it three hard times, paused, then tapped twice. Probably some secret knock they had, definitely more effective than hoping to blow it off the hinges.

A few seconds later the door swung open, and she greeted whoever opened it and stepped aside to grant her access. Without a word, Da Squad followed laying down everything in the room breathing. The mission complete, they began to collect their bonuses. The deal was, their employer only wanted the targets eliminated. Any money, drugs, or whatever else they found on the job was all theirs.

Ten minutes later, they were in the two trucks, loaded up with the money, drugs, jewelry, guns, and everything else they found of value, heading away from a rapidly burning building.

By time any emergency vehicles responded, there'd be nothing

but ashes and dirt. Skiddlez sat in the passenger seat, and smiled

at another job well done. Then placed the call to relay the mes-

sage to their employer.

"It's done." "Very good, you never disappoint do you.

Check the account I set up for you as usual. I'll be in touch."

With that, the call was disconnected. Skiddlez smiled & relaxed

his head back on the seat, as his thoughts drifted back to the day

he was approached by Da Squad's new employer...

16

It had been weeks since he'd dropped Baby G off at her crib, and his mind was still reeling. First, he loses Tasha, then before he has time to figure out the shit that transpired between him & Baby G… She's taken from him as well. Even though she was still alive, her absence seemed to hit him just as hard.

The high from the massacre had long been worn off, and he was looking for anything to numb the pain. He sat in his living room with a half empty bottle of Maker's Mark, and a loaded gun spinning in front of him on the table. He popped another pill, and chased it with a shot & a toke on his stick of Moonrocks.

He was about to spin his burner again, like a game of spin the bottle, when he thought he heard something on the side of the house. "Da fuck? Lemme find out there's a possum or some shit going through my trash, I got something hot for that ass." He grabbed his burner off the table and stood to go investigate. Before his hand could grip around the doorknob, it came crashing in stumbling him back a couple feet.

Instincts immediately kicked in as a masked man appeared gun in hand. *Bak-a Bak-a*. He squeezed off two shots, one to the chest, the other catching the intruder in the nose. He saw the shadow of more figures moving outside, and dove into the kitchen, just as shots came ripping through his back window. Protected by the counters, he low crawled to the back hallway.

The crunching of glass let him know that the assailants had entered the house. He slid behind a door and waited quietly, controlling his breathing, listening for any tell of the enemy's whereabouts. The popping of joints and bones alerted him to one right around the corner... He waited till they were all the way in the room, and isolated from however many more were in the house, before he pistol whipped him on the back of the head.

The body dropped like a sac of potatoes. Before he could recover, Skiddlez was on his back & twisting his neck in a quick motion, disconnecting his vertebrae. The door creaked behind him, and he rolled into the bathroom at his left. With a quick pivot, he spun and threw hot lead in the direction of the door. Wild shots rang out in return as the body collapsed.

When they stopped, he peaked out to confirm the other body down. Gurgles escaped the body as he held his hands to a bullet wound on his neck. Skiddlez walked up and ended his torment. Adrenaline coursing through his veins, he scooped the Mp5 out of the attacker's hands, threw caution to the wind, and ran into the hallway squeezing the trigger. He caught a man by surprise waiting around the corner, and glimpsed another high tailing it in the opposite direction.

"Uhn-uhn muthafucka, don't run now! Ya'll niggas came up in my shit askin for this, now you gon just quit. Where's ya follow through, huh?" He smiled like a lunatic as he gave chase. He found him about to hit the side of the house and escape. Without hesitation, he riddled his back with shots. "Gotta be quicker than that!" He spat, walking up on the fallen attacker and putting a few more bullets in him.

Screeching tires brought his attention away from the corpse. He made it to the front yard in time to glimpse a black van hitting a left up the street, and out of sight. A ringing sound arose from inside his house, and he followed it to one of the bodies in the hallway. A quick search and he came up with a ringing cell phone. He answered it and listened intently. "Very nice Thomas, your application is now complete. You've performed allot better than I expected, and with absolutely no training. I am impressed."

Skiddlez looked at the phone perplexed, "Who in da fuck is this, and what you talkin about application? Matta fact, how you even know my fuckin name?" A laugh came through the phone, "There is much I know Thomas. Such as, I know it was you and your friends that crashed that funeral. That was a very bold move, and put you on the radar of some important people." "I don't know what the fuck your talkin about."

"Of course you don't, and that is only another plus on your application. Tell me Thomas, how are you feeling right now? I bet that adrenaline in your system's better than any of those drugs you choose to abuse. There's nothing like that after-kill sensation, is there?" Skiddlez remained quit for a second as he realized the truth of the man's words.

"I still don't know what the fuck your talking about, and you still haven't told me who the fuck you are? And what the fuck is this application you keep talking about? You sent these people to my house to kill me, now you acting like I'm applying for some job. Typa shit is you on, whoeva da fuck you is?"

Another laugh, "Who I am isn't important right now. Those men were a part of your test, and you passed with fly-ing colors. My organization could use good men like you. How would you like to have access to that feeling your feeling now, on regular, and be greatly compensated for it as well?" Intrigued, he couldn't help asking, "Let's say I was interested, how much we talkin?"

"Each job will vary, but I can promise you nothing less than $20,000 apiece. Assuming you get your friends to come on board. I appear to now be five guys shorter than I was before your application." The wheels now turning in his head in over-drive, "Shit twenty racks a piece at least huh? Let me take it up with my peoples and get back to you. How exactly do I reach you?"

"You've got three days to decide, and I'll contact you. By the way, my apologies for the mess at your house. Clean up crew is on the way. They'll take care of everything, and the damages to the place as well. Also, don't worry about the authorities, we have that taken care of as well. It's been a pleasure."

The meeting wit Da Squad went about how he expected...

"You shittin me right, he said at least 20 racks a piece per job?" D-Money had dollar signs in his eyes. "You trust this mu-fucka?" Jo-Jo asked from between his girl's legs as she bolted down his braids.

"My nigga, I don't trust nobody outside Da Squad other than my T-Jones. Still this about business, and from what I seen so far he got the pull. I mean look around, not only did the crew come through and make them bodies disappear & any trace they coulda left, instead of just fixin the damages, the nigga done upgraded my shit."

Everybody's eyes cast over all the new furniture & appliances, and other improvements as their heads nodded in agreement. "You already know, if you in, then I got your back." Ivory stated, forever loyal to the bone. Skiddlez gave him a nod of appreciation & respect. "I'm sayin though, we don't know shit about this person. He calls on some Morphius shit, and we supposed to just run around knockin heads for him? This sum-bitch could be a FED, or even a white supremacist tryna get us to pull some Reagan shit..."

D-Money cut him off, "Mayne it's a twenty-rack minimum, as long as we getting the money, I don't give a fuck who he is. And the fuck you talkin about pull some Reagan shit?" Trackz looked at him like he was from a different planet, "Are you serious right now D? Please tell me your fuckin wit me right." D-Money's face showed he wasn't. Trackz shook his head and sighed at his boy's ignorance.

"Aight short version, Ronald Reagan was our president that started the crack epidemic in the hood as a way to try and population control minorities you could say. Fucked us up bad too, it was deemed the term Reaganomics. It wasn't until their rich little daughters and sons started taking trips to the hood and bringing the problem back to suburban door steps, that they claimed it was a problem. Blaming us of course, and started the war on drugs.

Anyways, bruh, you don't get it. You say you don't care who

he is as long as you get paid, but all money ain't good money. As soon as something goes wrong, or him and whatever organization he works for have no more use for us. They could issue the same kill order on us, and play it off by blasting our faces on TV as terrorist or some shit. And that's just one scenario."

Skiddlez sat back listening to his team weighing in. He couldn't help but smile at Trackz's comments, because he had also pondered the same thing the night before. He could always count on him to bring some knowledge & logic into a situation. Even D couldn't argue wit him, he just nodded his head at his boy's view.

Skiddlez turned and looked at Roscoe, who met his gaze, "My nigga, you already know. I'd body niggas for $20. Just like the man told you, that feeling alone is payment for me. So if you in, I'm right next to you." Skiddlez nodded, and took a second to contemplate everyone's words before speaking. "Aight Jo-Jo, Trackz, I definitely hear ya'll, and if ya'll really ain't feelin dis shit then we don't do it. You know it's all or nothing wit Da Squad, so just say the word."

Jo-Jo looked up at Gina, and she gave him a silent nod letting him know she supported his decision. "You know I'm down dawg, till the wheelz fall off." Trackz sighed, "Bro you know I'm in, I just wanna make sure being in don't take us out, ya feel me. We gotta have all our bases covered wit shit like this."

Skiddlez agreed. "And your absolutely right my nig. That's why the first chance we get, you gon dig up everything on this muthafucka and whoever it is he work for. We make sure we get enough shit on them, so that when they try to pull the rug from under us, we holdin the ropes to the nooses around they necks." Trackz smiled, "Now you speakin my language." Prissy cleared her throat, and everybody's head snapped in her direction. She had been so quiet off in the corner listening, that they almost forgot she was there.

"I just wanna say something. Ya'll niggaz done turned

real savage lately, and I know it's about to get worse once ya'll accept this job. You'll gon be out there on the front lines, and whoever this is will be focused on ya'll. I just want ya'll to re-member ya'll got some down ass bitches on Da Squad too. On some chess shit use your queens as a secret weapon if you ever need us. They'll never expect us for anything, and they'll never see us coming. Just cuz Baby G ain't around, don't mean the bitches can't get down."

With that, the decision had been made. Just as promised, three days after the first contact, he got in touch with him. Upon hearing they were on board, he created bank accounts for each of them, then sent them off to a grueling six week train-ing camp, espionage tactics & scenarios, rescue, maneuvers, and more. They'd done about six jobs for him since then, and each had acquired little over a quarter mill in their accounts.

17

Skiddlez snapped out of his thoughts as they pulled up to the driveway of their safe house, a nice 3-story house out in the burbs on the outskirts of the city. It had a room for each of them, even though they all had their own cribs. It was where they came to decompress after every mission, and they all stayed at least 24 hrs in case of any issues or repercussions from the unseen & unknown.

Everyone hopped out carrying bags into the house, and keeping their eyes open for anything out of place until they were all safely locked in the crib. Everyone went straight to the living room and sat quietly as Trackz pulled out his laptop & began typing away. After a minute, he nodded his head, then passed it to Skiddlez, who did the same. After the laptop had made it's rounds and everyone confirmed, they finally relaxed and fell into their normal routines.

Before anything, they always made sure everyone had received their payment for the job. Each had just witnessed a 45 rack increase in their accounts, which did wonders for their spirits. Now they all wore smiles on their faces as they got comfortable. The girls began handing out drinks and rolled blunts to everyone. Each lit their loud sticks to take to the head, and let the euphoric effects take over.

D-Money grabbed the bags of money they acquired, then he & Prissy got to counting. Ivory & Roscoe collected all the weapons and gear, then began breaking them down and cleaning them. Skiddlez turned the game on the T.V., pushed mute, then powered up the stereo and played some music. After he found the track he wanted, he grabbed the bags with the product they found in the safe, and separated them to determine the quantity & quality.

Jo-Jo & Gina grabbed the last two bags that contained the jewelry and other valuables the squad had collected from the hit. As they laid them out, they grabbed the most valuable items first and handed them to Trackz so he could price check them online. "Damn, this gotta be how Christopher Columbus felt when he discovered America!" Jo-Jo cried out holding up a platinum bracelet with a giant glistening world rotating in the center of it.

Trackz made his signature annoyed *sigh* he makes when he hears something he considers ignorance. "Mayne, ain't no damn Christopher Columbus discovered America." Jo-Jo rolled his eyes & sucked his teeth, "Bro, what typa shit you talkin now? Where the fuck was you at in history class, you musta been sleep through that lesson huh?"

It was Trackz turn to suck his teeth, "Oh you mean the same lesson that told you he simply sat down with the Indians over a peaceful dinner of turkey, then they just gave us all of their land out of the kindness of their hearts? Come on bro, what that even sound like? Please tell me when we Americans have ever taken anything without war and violence, much less a whole continent. Regardless, America was discovered long before Christopher Columbus stumbled upon it.

You obviously never heard of Abubakari II. He was an African who's tribe had conquered the lands in Africa from the sea to the dessert. He ended up on a ship to find his men he'd sent out previously, but hadn't returned. He stumbled upon America and the tribe caught itself in wars with the locals that led to trading and more.

Plenty of evidence has been recovered to testify to this as facts, such as terracotta & giant heads carved out of massive basilic stone balls, with undeniable African features. Some were discovered right here in Georgia. Not to mention the countless artifacts and skeletons from here to South America. White folks wanted to keep this secret to control and oppress us. They already feared us, and were trying to tame us through miseducation and Christianity. They knew they'd have no hope if we found out we were the true inheritants of the world and had been rulers for thousands of years, so they tried to erase our entire history."

Jo-Jo's mouth was open as he stared at Trackz with a look of disbelief mixed with anger. "No bullshit my nigga?" Trackz put his hand over his heart, "I bullshit you not my brother." Nobody talked for a minute while the knowledge Trackz had just dropped sunk in.

"Damn that's fucked up. White folks stay on some bullshit. Our people trapped in poverty killin each other for a meal, and we really supposed to be runnin all this shit." Roscoe spat. "Hell yeah, labeling us inferior beings, and throwing us scraps. Then dumbing us down with limited education and drugs, while they guard the truth for their own personal gain. That's some beyond fucked up shit." Prissy added.

"This is true, but we can't put all the blame on them, because we allowing them to do it. As many of us as there is, we could easily take our rightful dues back if we could just get our shit together and work together." Trackz responded, Skiddlez sat back puffin on his stick and listening to Da Squad. He definitely agreed with them about how messed up it was, the way their people were oppressed.

Still though, for some reason he couldn't stop his mind from drifting to something completely off topic. He found himself thinking this very thought allot. Loosing Tasha had hurt bad, then Baby G leaving right after what happened fucked him up even more. Now as Da Squad seemed to be getting richer than they could have ever imagined... His mind kept at the one thing missing, his thoughts coming back to the same repetitive question. "I wonder how Baby G is doing?"

18

"Eccc-xcuuse me... Umm hell-ooo. Did you hear what I said, or was I out here just talking for my health?!" The woman's tone finally got Baby G's attention. "I'm sorry, what was that?" The woman sucked her teeth & huffed in frustration before continuing. "I saa-iid, make sure my fries are fresh!" "Sure thing, your order will be right up." She responded after relaying the message to her co-workers.

Her focus was still on the three men that had just entered the restaurant. Her gut told her what was up the minute she saw them crossing the parking lot. Two of em wore red T-Shirts with black jeans, while the third was dressed in all black. That was the one who approached her register with a serious look plastered on his face. His two partners stood a step behind with matching looks as they eyed the surroundings.

"May I help you?" She asked, pretending like she didn't notice their demeanor. The man locked his intense gaze on her, "Yeah, you can help me to all the papa in that register to start with!" His deep baritone voice made her take in the rest of his features. He stood about 5'11, light skinned, covered in tatts from his drop-down braids to his fingertips.

Without missing a beat, she responded calmly with, "Would you like fries with that?" His face scrunched up for a second as he processed her words. She had to stifle a laugh, knowing that was probably the last thing he expected her to say. He looked back at his boys to make sure he wasn't trippin, and was met wit matching expressions. He remembered himself, and gave them a nod.

That's when they sprang into action pulling out weapons and shouting orders. The one in black trained his weapon on Baby G, "Oh bitch, you thought I was playing or something?" She looked at him unphased, "No I just figured that if you was gonna be robbin the place, you mine as well take some food wit you." It was his turn to check her out. His eyes wandered up and down her body, noticing that she hadn't even flinched when he trained his gun on her.

"What, you find yoself a comedian or something? Don't you know I could put some hot shit in you, while you tryna joke like we just playing in a movie or something." She leaned in closer on her elbows, "First of all, you ain't bout to shoot shit. Otherwise you wouldn't have ran up in here bare faced. Second, no I ain't no comedian. Ain't my style, though I do have my moments."

It was his turn to stifle a laugh, he had to admit that he was digging her style. He visibly relaxed, "Girl, everybody know these raggedy ass cameras don't work in this place. I could just as easily body everyone in this joint and ride off clean." She shrugged, "True, but there's an awfully lotta work to be putting in for some chump change. You da third niggaz to come up in this bitch."

The whole while they talking, the other two had been putting the place into chaos. One of em turned noticing the two conversating, "Juice, the fuck you over there doin, tryna get the bitch number or something?" Juice shot his boy the bird, "She say the muthafuckas already been rodded twice this month and ain't shit left up in dis bitch but a couple bills."

That seemed to piss the other one off and he jumped over the counter, then jammed the barrell of his gun into the side of her head. "The bitch probably lyin. Open up the fuckin register hoe, before I splatter yo shit all over the place!" Baby G snaked her neck and forcefully pushed the barrel out of her face, "Get that shit out my face before I take it then shove it up your ass and make some real shit come out ya mouth for probably the first time in ya life."

Juice couldn't stop the laugh from escaping this time, and

the look on his boy's face ain't help any. He looked over at him, and Juice just shrugged, "She's a trip ain't she." He noticed the look in his homies eyes and knew he'd have to take control, "Go find the supervisor or something and make him open up the safe. I'll handle thug misses here." He hesitated for a second, then turned to do what he was told. He turned his attention back to Baby G, "You know he's a hothead right, you don't know how close you almost came to getting what you was askin for."

She rolled her eyes, "Yeah whatever. Anyways, Juice huh? Why they call you that, you sposed to be Bishop or something?" He smiled, "Oh you on a roll today huh? They call me that, because I got it." She smiled back, "That you do... that you do." He had to admit that he was feelin her, "So you know my name, what's yours?" Baby G pressed the button on the register for the till to shoot out. She pulled a $20 bill, then wrote something on it and put it back with the others.

"Tell ya boi I don't preciate being called a liar." Then she handed the drawer to him. He looked in it to see a few bills that probably added up to a buck fifty. He pulled out the $20 first and read the name & number on it before folding it up, then placing it in his pocket. The rest he handed to his homie who had been relieving everyone in the restaurant of all their wallets, purses, & valuables.

Just then Livewire returned from the back wit a salty look on his face, "Mayne, wasn't shit in that funky ass safe. Weak ass nigga ain't even had a pistol in there." Baby G shot him an I told you so look. "Welp Baby G, looks like we'll be taking all the sandwiches and fries ya'll got ready. Throw some apple pies up in da mix too. Ya'll want anything else?"

Livewire sucked his teeth, still poutin about the situation. "Yeah mayne, gimmie a vanilla shake." "Make mine strawberry." Said the other one. "Fuck it, make mine chocolate." Juice added with a wink. After getting everything, they headed for the exit. Before hitting the door. Juice turned and gave Baby G a look that said he'd be seeing her again. She returned one that said she was counting on it.

Two hours later, her shift ended and she was walking out the doors to her cousin Kyra waiting in her Acura. "Sup cuz, damn why you always come out of there like it's a slave ship or something?" She greeted playfully. "Sup cuz, and because you know damn well that job's bullshit." Baby G responded wit mock attitude.

"You sure right about that. I still can't believe you chose to return there every day. Once I graduated, I was oh too happy to high tail it up outta there and never look back." Kyra responded scrunching up her face at the memory. "Yeah, well we ain't all blessed with your opportunities princess. With Mrs. Higgins having me blackballed, this is apparently the only place I can get hired. I still don't understand what that bitches problem is, hoe don't even know me."

"Yeah, she definitely got it out for you for some reason." Kyra agreed as she pulled out the parking lot. Mrs. Higgins was the principal at the high school and for some reason, had pull like the town gatekeeper. If anybody under 30 wanted a job, they had to go through her first. "Anyways, if it wasn't for this job, where would I get all my excitement from? Can you believe we got robbed again today?!"

Kyra's head snapped towards her so fast, she had to regain control of the car. "Get the fuck outta here, that's like the fifth time this month. I'm surprised there's even any money left there to take. I bet Peter's little bitch ass ain't did shit neither. He needs to supervise some damn security up in there, always tryna act like he somebody."

"Girl please, you know his punk ass was hiding in the back somewhere the whole time. All for the best anyway, because it gave me a chance to get to know one of the robbers." She proceeded to tell her cousin how everything went down. When she was finished, her cousin couldn't do anything but laugh. "Bitch you a mess, I can't believe you done wrote your number down on some money a nigga was robbin you for."

"Wasn't my money he was takin, & he deserved something for all that trouble he went through for nothin." They both had a good laugh at that. "You crazy as hell cuz, but on some real shit if you want some real money, you should take Dante up on his offer. Then you can have plenty of excitement, and you'll probably get robbed less. Shit at least it'll make sense when you do." Dante's Kyra's boyfriend, and also the plug. When Baby G came to town, he told her he had heard of her and offered to put her on.

As tempting as the offer was, she made a promise & she planned to keep it. "I appreciate it, but I already told ya'll that I'm trying to do the right thing this time round." Kyra shrugged her shoulders, "Suit yourself, guess I can't do nothin but respect it." Baby G rested her head back on the seat and let her mind wander. Life had definitely been different since she'd come to stay here. Doing the right thing was no easy task.

She had set out to get her G.E.D. immediately. After bust-ing her ass day in and day out, she was filled with pride when she achieved it. Unfortunately, the real world came knockin immediately after. She went from no money to slow money, and most the time slow money felt like no money. To do the right thing, she seemed to have to sacrifice everything she loved.

She hadn't been shopping in months. If she wasn't riding with her cousin, she was either walking or on public transportation. Worst of all was the bedroom, and most days she felt like she was living the same day over and over. To stop from backsliding, she'd always recall the conversation she had with her mother and the promise she made. Then she'd remember that she could always be locked up or in the ground. To finish it off she'd motivate herself that this was all temporary, and the harder she worked the better things would get.

The car stopped, and she pulled from her thoughts to find they were pulled up to a gas pump. "There any Swishers left at the crib?" She asked being reminded by the store. "Naw, I'm pickin up some now. You want anything else?" She shook her head no, then got out to pump the gas while her cousin went into the store. When they both hopped back in & were ready to pull off, a car swung in front of them blocking their path.

As Kyra leaned on the horn, Baby G instinctively reached for the glove box. Another car slid in and parked by the driver door. Recognizing the vehicle before the person even hopped out, she rolled her eyes and relaxed. "Oh great, this day just keeps getting better and better. This clown just don't know when to give up." A short pudgy dark-skinned guy appeared from around the driver's side rockin a starched white tall T, over some pressed jeans, and some white on white Forces.

He smiled to reveal a row of golds bellow his Gucci shades. "Well well well, if it ain't my future baby mama, and my future ex-wife. I almost converted to Muslim just so I could marry both of you... But I just couldn't give up the pork." He laughed at his own joke, and his boys joined in. "Mayne Lil Mic, the fuck you want. There's only so many ways a bitch can tell you No, and leave us the fuck alone." Baby G yelled out the window.

Undeterred he just laughed, "Well that's good, because when you've run out of ways then all that's left is to say yes. Then daddy's gon make everything all better for the both of ya'll." Kyra & Baby G looked at each other, then burst out laughing. "Nigga please, if you don't get yo midget Charlie Murphy lookin ass away from my car..." Kyra said, "Daaarkneesss everybody, Daarrkknneesss!" Baby G followed, and they burst out laughing again.

"Yeah whatever, this darkness'll make you go night night wit one shot. Why don't you come and get a taste?" He was now leaning in the window, his gold chain swinging in the car. An "R" was encrusted on it in diamonds to represent his little clique that called themselves the Ruffians. Two of which were standing outside laughing like their leader was doing stand-up.

"Pass!" Baby G spat, giving him a little twist of the hand

for emphasis. "Yeah whatever, fuck all that. I stopped ya'll to invite ya'll to the party I'm throwin this Friday. My nigga just got out the pen, and we gon do it real big for him. It's only right that I personally invite the two baddest bitches in the city." He dropped his glasses so they could see his eyes and winked.

"Boy what makes you think we'd ever get caught at one of yo watered down ass parties?" His face got real tight for a second, then relaxed. "True, it ain't gon be like the killer parties your used to back home." He shot back. Kyra felt the tension building in the car and thought to act fast, "Look, we busy Friday, but write down the address and if we can steal some time we'll stop by." This seemed to do the trick as the smile returned back to his face, and he wrote down the info.

"Aight you do that, and tell lil mama over there to leave her itchy trigger finger at home. You think she'd be tired of funerals by now." Before either could respond, he blew a kiss then was heading to his whip. Two honks, and the cars rolled out. "oooo, I hate that purple muthafucka. He swear he somebody." Baby G vented, unclenching her fists. Kyra shook her head and aimed the car towards the crib.

"I don't know why you let that nigga get to you. Shake him off cuz, he harmless. He just another horny lil mutt running the streets tryin to smell some ass." Baby G knew she was right, but there was just something about him that rubbed her the wrong way. Ever since she had come to town, he seemed to always be popping up everywhere sweatin her. When they pulled up to the house, she was just ready to change out of her work clothes and put one in the air.

By time she got out the shower, her other cousin Daysia was sittin on the end of Kyra's bed. Her favorite artist Drake was bumpin out the speakers attached to her phone, and she was singin & dancing along in her own little world. Daysia was the little cousin. She was about 5'6, real thick with that rebel style shaved hair that few could pull off. Yet she did it flawlessly, and it matched her personality. She always had this positive outlook on things, claimin she was a rebel with a cause.

"What's up trick, I'm surprised you ain't in here bumpin some Jill Scott or Lauren Hill." She stopped dancing, and smiled when she saw Baby G. "Hey girl, and naw today I'm playin my husband's music. Gotta support him so he can bring his ass home to mama." She said the last couple words wit a lil twist and dip. "Bitch you crazy as hell." Baby G laughed as she snatched a blunt off the bed in front of Kyra, then found a seat.

Sparking it up, they effortlessly fell into conversation about their days. Of course Kyra couldn't help bring up Juice. "Let me find out you done finally found somebody you was interested in up here!?" Daysia screeched wit a wide grin on her face. Apparently Baby G's silence was all the confirmation she needed to continue. "Yes girl, it's written all over your face. I thought for a second I was gonna have to find this Skiddlez nigga for you and bring him up here." At the mention of Skiddlez's name, Baby G's mind shot off in a completely different direction.

Her cousins were too caught up in their excitement to realize, "Really Daysia, you just gonna encourage her, the nigga was in there robbin her. She lucky he didn't shoot her for workin in that broke ass establishment." Daysia rolled her eyes and let the smoke out she was holdin in. "So what, atleast he got some ambition. He could just'a been another bum ass dude tryna live off a woman. Nope, instead he was goin out and tryna get it at any means necessary. On top of that, it mighta brought him straight to his true love."

That brought Baby G back, "There you go, always talkin that love shit. I ain't even been out wit da nigga, and you already ringin wedding bells. Bitch I been done told you dat ain't my style no way. Can't a bitch just want some dick from a real nigga?" They shared a laugh at that. They carried on like that for the rest of the night, smokin and clownin. Her cousins were the only reason she was makin it, without snapping, in her new environment. They were close enough to be her sisters, and were her support team to keep her on track.

19

Days later, Kyra had hit her line to let her know she wouldn't be able to scoop her form work, because she was caught up with Dante handlin business. Baby G was used to this, and didn't mind. On days like this, she'd either walk back, or ride the bus. She never thought she'd be on public transportation, but she quickly adapted, and learned her way around. Leaving out of work, she decided that today was one of those days to walk.

She put her earbuds in and pressed play on her playlist on her IPhone. She'd taken the route so much, that her legs took her on autopilot as she zoned out to the music and her thoughts. The sound of a car horn brought her back to her surroundings, though she didn't pay it much attention because thirsty ass niggas was always doing that shit when she was walking.

Instead of wasting her time cussing them out like she liked to do sometimes. She just cut through a back alleyway to remove herself from the main street traffic. Soon though, she thought she heard the sound of tires over gravel behind her. Instead of turning around, she picked her pace up and slid her hand closer to her purse where she kept her switchblade. When she heard the car doors slam, she immediately wished she would have packed her pistol.

She turned around with her hand in her purse, to face her pursuers. Seeing Lil Mic and two of his Ruffian lapdogs spread out in front of her, sent a wave of rage coursing through her. "Stalk much nigga?" He smiled and held his hands up to his heart like he was hurt. "Aww don't be that way. I see a beautiful woman walking by herself, and I couldn't resist lending my assistance. Why don't you hop in and I'll give you a ride where you need to go." He licked his lips as his eyes traveled up and down her frame.

"Nigga please, like I'd go anywhere with you. Ever... and

you keep looking at me like that and you gon loose an eye." The three men laughed, then Lil Mic nodded his head and his boys moved to surround her. "Now see, why you gotta always be disrespectful to me. I show you nothin but kindness since you came into my city, and this the way you repay me. You do know, I always get what I want right?"

He rose off the car and took a step towards her. Baby G's hand rose out the purse wit the blade in hand. "Uhn – Uhn nigga, keep ya muthafuckin distance pussy ass nigga!" He only paused for a second, "Mayne, what the fuck you gon do with that. I ain't ticklish hoe." He sneered, then continued to close in on her. She tried to turn and keep all three in her line of sight, but they had her surrounded.

A quick glance of his eyes over her left shoulder hinted her to his boy's movements. She swiveled in his direction, blade slashing out and connecting with cotton and meat. "Aaahhh, you fuckin bitch!" She turned slashing in a circle to keep them at

FOR BETTER OR WORSE

bay. The sight of their boy getting cut made them both hesitate but only for a second.

Lil Mic pulled his pistol from his waist, "Bitch put the fuckin knife down. Don't make this harder than it has to be. We just gon have a lil fun then you can go on your way. You keep fighting it though, and you gon find out one of the reasons they call us Ruffians." Unphased by the gun, she spit in his direction, "Fuck all three of you lil dick niggas, try and see what happens."

The focus she gave him was enough to keep her distracted. The world seemed to go all white, the next she knew she was stumbling towards a wall. By time she realized one of his goons had punched her in the side of the head, they were all over her. Her arms were pinned to the ground as her shirt was being lifted. She kicked and bucked, but to no avail. "Get the fuck off me!" She yelled.

Instead of complying, she felt her pants being yanked down her legs exposing her panties. "Mmmm, something told me you had a nice fat ass pussy." Lil Mic said, laying his burner

on the ground as he started fidgeting with his belt buckle.

"Psych, Shade, hold this bitch still for me. Matta fact, take that

shirt off so we can enjoy those titties bouncing while I do my

thing." To take the shirt over her head, they had to release one

of her hands. She used that second to grab the gun on the waist

of the one called Shade, that she felt as he was holding her down.

Without pulling it all the way out of his waistband, she

squeezed the trigger twice. He instantly fell backwards in pain.

Going with his momentum, and using the moment of shock the

other two were in, she dove for Lil Mic's gun and came up with it

in her hand. "Stay the fuck back! I swear to God I'll plug both of

you niggas like ya bitch ass lil homie over there!"

Shade was doubled over from taking two to the gut. She

knew he wasn't gonna recover from his injuries, so when Psych

decided to defy her and reach for his waist, she turned and put a

bullet in Shade's head to make her point. "I swear to God, if you

move another muscle I'll send ya'll chasin after him to the Devil's doorstep." Lil Mic mugged her, but didn't move a muscle. "You don't even know how much you just fucked up bitch. You just started some shit, I hope you can finish."

Baby G kept backing up, keeping her pistol moving back and forward between her targets. "I didn't start this shit. I been tryin to stay away from this shit. I swear on my mother though, If you keep pushin me... I WILL finish it." When she felt like she had backed up far enough out of range, she turned and ran for the end of the alleyway. As she was coming to the end of it, a bullet whizzed by her head and into the brick wall next to her. She ducked and sent some shots back.

Lil Mic had grabbed Shade's gun, now he & Psych were both chasing her guns blazing. Baby G knew she couldn't outrun them straight up once they got to the street, yet she had to try. Using the corner of the building as cover, she sprinted down the sidewalk, mind working overtime on a plan. A car skidded next to her and her heart dropped. Thinking it was the Ruffians having jumped inside the car instead of giving chase on foot, she turned to send as many shots through the window before the inevitable happened.

When her eyes locked on the driver though, shooting was the last thing on her mind. "Don't just stand there girl, jump in." Juice stood with a gun pointed over the roof of his car, in the direction of the alley. When Psych came skidding around the corner, Juice let off a few rounds sending him diving back into the alleyway. Needing no more incentive, Baby G ran to the passenger's side and jumped in. Juice let off a few more rounds for good measure, then got in and floored the peddle. Speeding away from the scene.

Ignoring the chaos of the horns as he cut cars off swerving in & out of traffic on the two-lane street, his eyes transitioned from the rear & side mirrors to the road ahead. Occasionally he would steal a glance at Baby G, who was just staring outside the passenger window clutching the burner tight. After being sure they weren't being chased, he slowed down and blended with surrounding vehicles as to not attract attention from the laws.

Seeing she was still zoned out, he broke the silence. "You aight ma?" She didn't respond or even show any signs that she'd heard him. Her mind was going over what had just happened, and almost happened. She was torn between being visibly shaken, and outraged. "Ol trash ass niggas! They run around stuntin, pretending like they bossin or something talkin bout "My Town". Yet they was tryna take some pussy from a bitch in a alleyway!" She suddenly let out.

"Yeah dey weak as fuck for dat shit. That nigga Mic ain't nothin but a spoiled lil bitch anyways. He feel like the streets s'posed to be his birth right or sum'n cuz his peeps used to be plugged in way back when." Juice reiterated. Baby G rolled her eyes, "Them niggaz don't know shit about bein plugged in. Fake ass movie gangstas got they ass squashed where I'm from."

Juice wanted to ask where it was she was from, but figured it wasn't the best time to be getting into all of that. "True, but fuck dem niggas. You ain't answer my question. You aight ma?" he said instead. Baby G looked over at him, and noticed how fresh he was lookin & remembered how attractive he was. Then another emotion washed over her as she realized her pants were still undone, her shirt was torn, and she didn't even want to think of what her hair and face looked like. Trying not to show the embarrassment, she loosened her grip on the gun she was death clutching up until then, and slid it into her purse.

"Yeah I'm straight... I appreciate you stopping and helping me out." She replied while buttoning her pants and trying to fix herself as discreetly as possible. "No problem ma, though trouble seems to find you allot huh?" He said smirking at her sideways. Again her eyes traveled from his head full of waves, down to the print in his pants where she staggered for a second. "Story of my life actually, and I see your timing's actually been improving."

He raised an eyebrow, "How you figure that?" This time

she did the smirking, "Well the first time we met was nothing short of the right place, wrong time. Though this time round was definitely right place right time." They both smiled at that. "I don't know, that first time I was pretty fuckin hungry. So I could easily say that was also the right time wit all the food you hooked me up with." Laughter filled the vehicle, and Baby G finally felt herself relax.

They shared a comfortable moment of silence as their thoughts took off. Unwarranted, her mind went back to the alley & focused on a detail that had escaped her. She searched her purse, and sure enough her switchblade was missing. Though she had come up on a glock for the trade, she wasn't too happy about leaving a weapon at the same place she had left a body. Damn, and she'd been doing the good girl thing so well lately. "So… where you want me to take you?" Juice asked hesitantly.

As much as she was feeling him, she wasn't yet comfortable showin him where she lay her head. She thought about the scenario and said fuck it. Three busta ass niggas had almost

taken it, so what's the harm if somebody she didn't mind at all

tryna take it. She hadn't had no dick since that night wit Skid-

dlez. So if this nigga tried to play, she might be the one taking

something. She glanced at his print unconsciously again as she

replied, "Wherever's clever."

20

"Is that a fuckin castle!?" D-Money's eyes were damn near bulging out of his head. "The target's inside. It's just like we practiced so get ready." Skiddlez said tryna down play the situation and focus the team. "Naw but my nigga, that's a real live fuckin castle!" D-Money continued not havin any of Skiddlez misdeirection.

D-Money wasn't the only one, the whole team stared out the tinted windows, of the all black hummer, in awe. They had seen it through the pictures & videos with the mission, and studied it in & out. Still, seeing the massive structure in front of them was a whole different story. Skiddlez gave everyone a minute to take it in, and get themselves together, then it was game time.

While Trackz sent a drone in to survey the perimeter, the rest of Da Squad got suited up. There were so many high trained men inside this building guarding the target, that this mission had to be handled with stealth & finesse. Given the all clear, they set out to the East Side of the castle where security had a blind spot. Using air pressured graplin guns, they climbed to the roof taking out the two unsuspecting guards posted, into the castle they went.

They each carried their own state of the art weapons. Ivory was like a giant kid on Christmas waiting to play with his. He carried a assault rifle that had a 4' screen on it that showed everything the camera on the barrel picked up. The settings could be changed to infrared, night vision, and more. That wasn't the best thing about it though. Somehow you could bend the gun around corners that you can see and shoot around them. With the silencer connected, he was on some real 007 shit.

Needless to say, he led the way through most of the compound, clearing a path with ease. Jo-Jo carried a device that set a perimeter, took a picture of everything in front and around, then projected a hologram image making all inside the perimeter basically invisible. This they used in the heavily guarded areas to sneak by unnoticed. They rounded a corner thinking they were safe, when a guy in a turban stepped out of the room and straight into their perimeter.

Everyone froze and stared at each other. Just when the man put together what was going on and opened his mouth, Roscoe slid up behind him and slit his throat, silencing him forever. D-Money had goggles that could see through walls, and any material known to man, by toggling with a push of a button. To combo he had two earpieces in that could pick up sound for 30 feet in any direction, and through solid material as well. He took a peek through the wall of the room the men emerged from.

Seeing it was clear, they dragged the body back in where it came from, and continued on. A minute later they were mere feet away from where the target was said to be. D-Money confirmed the target was where he was supposed to be, "Ya'll won't believe this though. He's in there with three bad bitches that look like Serena Williams, Kim Kardashian, & Mariah Carey. The hoes is given it to each other more than they given it to him... Oh lawd, they got a long ass double sided dildo and they taken every inch... Hold on ya'll, why don't ya'll take a walk around the corner or something and give me a few minutes."

Skiddlez slapped him upside the head, "Stop playin bruh and get serious before somebody pop our tops." D-Money tried to sound serious, "Sorry boss." But his eyes were still glued to the wall. Shaking his head, Skiddlez set up for his turn to play. "Everyone keep watch. Remember, once I pull this trigger, all hell's gonna break loose. Getting in was the easy part, everyone stick together and let's get ghost in 90 seconds." They each nodded and took positions.

The room the target was in was encased in reinforced bullet proof glass, and the doors were reinforced steel. A security system was set up with AI target guns that could recognize intruders not registered to the system, then cut em down to pieces. To make matters worse, the target had a device hooked to his heartbeat so that if it ever stopped, then the building would self-destruct. Talk about paranoid. Still, Da Squad knowing all of this in advance, came prepared.

Skiddlez set a device on the floor that would emit an EMP burst, disabling all electronics in the building except for theirs which were specifically guarded against for this purpose. He raised a specialized rifle that could lock-on to up to five targets, in which the bullets could find no matter where they ran or hid. The bullets contained diamond tips that rotated and cut through barriers by burrowing through, never losing the lock on their targets.

Now seeing what D-Money was seeing, it almost hurt to have to disrupt such a beautiful scenery. Never-the-less, when the gun confirmed a lock on all four targets, he prepared to pull the trigger, "Three, two, one." He counted down, pressed the button on the EMP, then pulled the trigger. As the four bullets dug their way through the walls, he watched as the ménage continued oblivious to the signs of everything around them shutting down.

It seemed Kim Kardashian's vibrator was the only thing that they noticed, as she removed it from her fat lips and banged it against her palm a few times. By her third slap against her palm, her head snapped back and her body slumped to the bed. The other three imitated her movements and slumped around her. "Target eliminated." Skiddlez confirmed.

"You literally just killed a wet dream bruh." D-Money said solemnly, sounding on the verge of tears. Ignoring him, they all took off in the direction they'd come. Figuring they'd already cleared the path coming in, they took off full speed. It wasn't till they hit a corner and came to face a force of seven heavily armed soldiers in their path, that they realized it wasn't gonna be that easy.

They dove back around the corner, just as the soldiers

opened fire. "Fuck, well so much for that way. Plan B, Trackz find us another way out." They laid down some suppressing fire to keep the soldiers back, then took off the other way led by Trackz's directions. A left, a right, down some stairs, another right, kill a few here, kill a few there. They knew every second still in the building was a worse situation to escape.

Ivory had just taken out a few guards around a corner, when some how they got flanked. Fighting two separate groups, they ended up separated. Skiddlez with Ivory, and the other three around a corner somewhere. "In there!" Ivory had kicked down a door, and was laying cover for Skiddlez to get through. When Skiddlez made it through, Ivory turned to follow, and felt two sharp pains enter his back, propelling him through the door.

"Aahhh shit, muthafuckas." Was all he said as he flew to the floor. "Ivory!" Skiddlez yelled, seeing his mans down he ex-pected the worse. He grabbed a hold of him, and felt the blood soaking his back. "Naw bro, hell naw. Please tell me you good my nigga. Ivory!" He cradled him, tryna gauge how bad he was hit. A second passed before he groaned, "Ahh, that shit hurt like a bitch. I'm straight though bro, nothin but a flesh wound." Skiddlez looked at the blood soaking his boy's back, then back at his eyes.

"A flesh wound my ass nigga, you bleeding everywhere. We gotta get you outta here, and to a doctor." Ivory shook his head and tried to pull Skiddlez away, "Nigga we in a whole nutha country on some assassin shit, fuck a doctor, let's just get back to the plane." Before Skiddlez could respond, he caught movement out of the corner of his eye. Turning to see the barrel of the soldier's gun pointed in his face. He knew he had got caught slippin. "Fuck it, real niggas gotta die sometime." Was all he said as he waited for the bullet to end his life.

Boom – Boom. The explosion was louder than he suspected, and couldn't help thinking that must be how it sounds when the bullets enter your brain. Then he realized he was still thinking. As he stared at the soldier, his whole left side seemed to glow red like hot magma had been poured on him, then another second later the body crumbled. "Yeah, but these real niggas ain't dyin today." Roscoe said brandishing his customized combat shotgun loaded with dragon rounds.

More shots rang out from the hallway. "Ya'll hurry up, we gotta get outta here. Now!" Jo-Jo yelled, "D, Come help me with Ivory!" Skiddlez yelled. "Naw I'm good, I can walk." Ivory said standing up stubbornly. They fought their way out the castle and back to the hummer. Trackz already had it idling and ready to go. They were moving before all the doors were shut. Ivory leaned his head back on the seat, "Uhn-uhn my nigga, don't close your fuckin eyes. Stay wit me." Skiddlez said wit worry lacing his voice. "Push this muthafucka Trackz!"

Knowing the situation, Trackz had already called ahead to the G4, and told the pilot to have the engines ready for immediate take off and somebody with medical experience on board. "Uh guys, they ain't letting shit go that easy." D-Money spoke, referring to the three jeeps appearing not far from their tail. "I got this." Roscoe said removing the heavy machine gun from the trunk area. "Just drive this muthafucka steady."

He rose up through the sunroof on some Rambo shit, yelling and lacin the vehicles wit bullets. One swerved and smashed into a tree, but the other two were relentless. Their passengers began to return fire of their own. "There should be a few grenades back there in the side panels." Trackz informed. Jo-Jo found them and wasted no time removing the pin and tossing it out the window. The explosion rocked the hummer, but blew up on the back-right side of one of the jeeps, sending it spiraling off the road.

"Uh... guys, hurry up. We're running out of time." A quick glance through the windshield showed the distant plane visible on the vacant air strip. Bullets smashed through the rear glass. The last vehicle wasn't giving up without a fight. Jo-Jo threw another grenade, and it expertly swerved around dodging the explosion. All the while, Roscoe was still letting off rounds through the roof. Skiddlez looked at Ivory and slapped him in the face, "I said stay the fuck awake. Don't make me fuck you up bro. I got a plan, but I need you to fight that shit while I do this." He simply smiled and nodded his head.

Skiddlez retrieved his gun and locked on to the driver of the last jeep. "Dodge this, bitch." The bullet ripped through the rear window, shattering it to pieces, and found it's mark. The jeep continued in pursuit for a second, then veered left off the road smashing into a giant boulder. A minute later they were screeching to a halt next to the plane. All loaded up, the plane took flight on a course back to the U.S.

21

"Mmmmm-mmm-mmm." Was all she could manage as her face was being forced down into the pillow. Tears came from her eys as she felt herself suffocating, combined with the relentless assault on her body. She struggled against the hand on her head, but it was too strong, seeming to push further the more she fought it. Her arms were useless, seeing as they were both tied behind her back.

On the verge of passing out, she managed to turn her head slightly to the right. Her lungs, that were screaming for oxygen, got a rush of relieving air at last. "Ooohhh shit, dis nigga tryna kill me!!!" She let out soon as her lungs refilled. Digging deep, she arched her back and tried to throw back what she was receiving. "Dat's all you got left? I told you I was gon murder this pussy. You mighta got that first round, but that's just because you caught me off guard with this good shit. Now I gotta get my get back." Juice taunted while his thick 9 ½ inches plunged deep into her gushing hole.

The way he was handling her had her juices flowing freely down her legs. The rough treatment turned her all the way the fuck on, and she could do nothing but admit he was doing his thing through some incoherent words. She gave up the fight, and just lay there taking the intense waves of pleasure he was sending through her as he hammered into her. Drool escaped the side of her mouth as she saw his length going in and out of her, glistening with her essence.

"Oooo shit girl, yo pussy tight as fuck. I feel like I'm diving into heaven." His words just coaxed her into another orgasm. Her natural lube only made the pussy feel 10 times better. He flipped her over so now that her arms were pinned behind her back. Pushing her knees to her chest he held on to the back of her legs and rocked into her love box. "Mmm-mmm-mhm, fuck dis pussy. Mmm, fuck yeah." Her eyes rolled in the back of her head as she felt herself nearing another orgasm.

"Shit I'm bout to cum again!" Her words coached him to the brink as well. He spread eagle her legs, and dug as deep as he could as they both released their juices together. Still holding her shaking legs, he collapsed on top of her, their tongues finding each other in between breathes. After getting his bearings, Juice hopped up with a smile on his face and smacked her on the ass. "Oww boy," she smiled back "Okay, you got that one fa sho."

He went to a drawer, and pulled a giant freezer bag out. Soon as he opened it, a strong odor filled the room. "Damn nigga, that shit funky than a muthafucka." Still smiling, he sat down and broke off some buds onto a rolling tray then handed it to her. He then proceeded to roll his own. Soon they were both holding lit sticks, and relaxin watching a Netflix movie, "Mm-mm-mmm, good weed and good dick. Keep this up and I might have to keep you around."

Baby G smiled while enjoying the euphoria of the combination. "Oh, keep me huh? Sho you right. I guess wit that golden, juicy muthafucka you carrying around, you got a whole kennel of dogs sniffing around." She pushed him playfully. "Boi please, real shit though, it's been a minute since a bitch been able to get her rocks off. I needed this shit more than I realized." She confessed.

He read her face and saw she was serious, and got serious himself. "To tell the truth, you ain't the only one. I mean it ain't been that long, but it's been a minute since it was like this." She understood what he was saying, and ain't take no offense. After a moment of silence, he spoke up, "You doin aight for real though? I mean… after that shit earlier, wit them fuck bois?"

She took a long drag of the blunt, then put it out. "Yeah I'm straight." She lied. She really didn't wanna talk, or think about it, especially on the high she was feeling at the moment. "What you was doin out that way anyways, let me find out you was stalkin a bitch." He gave her a goofy look, and playfully mush faced her. "Please, I just finished droppin my nigga off. I was gon go fuck wit my mans about some money moves, when I seen that loud ass uniform you be wearing. Ain't no mistaken that muthafucka."

He pointed to it layin on the floor, and they both laughed, "Fuck you nigga, but you damn sho right about that. So it was pure coincidence huh?" He looked her in the eyes, "I don't believe in coincidences, more like fate... Anyways, whatever it was, I know one thing fo sho. You may have that good good, but you see what I'm workin wit too. I damn sho ain't gotta stalk nobody." He got up and started doin the Dadd Dick scene from Baby Boy.

"Boy you crazy as hell!" She laughed, the weed was now taking full effect, and she started feeling herself tingling between her thighs. "Okay Jodie, scoreboard says 1-1 last time I checked." She seductively crawled to him and took him in her hand. Right before putting it in her mouth, she looked up into his eyes, "How bout best 2 out of 3."

–   –

"Bro I'm tellin you, something ain't right about these jobs." Trackz pleaded. "You damn right something's wrong... It shouldn't be this easy to make this much money!" D-Money interjected, prying a laugh from the rest of the group. They were now all back at the spot safely, deep into their after-job rituals, and each $5 Million richer. "No I'm for real about this bruh. At first I thought I was maybe just trippin a little too, but as the jobs kept coming I recognized an obvious trend in our targets."

He turned and made eye contact wit Skiddlez, "I know I'm not the only one who's noticed it neither." Skiddlez turned attention somewhere else, but couldn't deny what his mans was speakin. "Come on bro, so ya'll gon tell me I'm the only one who's noticed each one of our targets was black?" The room grew quite for a second as what he was saying soaked in. Though it wasn't news to most of them, who had been fighting their subconscious for the same realization.

"Mayne here you go. Everything gotta be some Black Panther caught up in a conspiracy shit. You trippin my nigga, the only color caught up in this shit is green." Roscoe spoke up with a slight slur already. Lately he'd had a bottle surgically attached to his hand. Skiddlez meant to address the issue before, but he knew his boy was just going through the stages of grief over his brother. "Yeah my nig, if anything it's probably just a coincidence. D-Money tried to reassure, though his voice wasn't very convincing itself.

"Naw mayne, this last one was the nail in the coffin for me. When we had got the picture of the target, something kept tuggin at me saying he looked familiar. Then when all the guards started showing up in Kufi wraps and garments, it clicked in. I ain't wanna believe it, so I started doin some research based off the resemblance. Sure enough it turns out our target was one of the illegitimate sons of Elijah Muhammad." He paused for a reaction, but got none.

Jo-Jo Shrugged, "Elijah who?" Trackz sighed in frustration, "Elijah Muhammad, the leader of the Nation Of Islam in America. Was self-proclaimed said to be a prophet/reincarnation of Allah. The one who recruited Malcolm X, ring any bells?" Prissy jumped up in excitement, "Oh yeah, wasn't that the guy that tried to kill Malcolm X because he had found out that the muthafucka was some major pedophile who was sleeping with a bunch of the teenage girls they were supposed to be helping?"

Trackz smiled, relieved that somebody actually knew something. "Yes exactly, though he wasn't just sleeping with these little girls. He was said to have fathered multiple children with them, then sent them away to keep his secret when they began demanding for money. Well, anyways, that last target was one of those illegitimate children."

Skiddlez moved around in his seat uncomfortably, "You're sure about this Trackz?" Trackz turned his laptop around showing a picture of their target with an attached article, "100% sure bro." Skiddlez glanced over the article confirming what was being spoken, then his hands were rubbing his temples as he processed everything. Roscoe rose up abruptly spilling his bottle all over the floor and sofa in the process, "Who gives a fuck if the nigga was the long-lost son of Obama, we got five million muthafuckin dollas a piece for dis pussies head. Fuck him AND his no pork eatin, child fuckin, Daddy!"

Ivory grunted from the couch behind them. The Doc had fixed him up. The bullets went straight through leaving behind minimum damage. Now Ivory was bandaged up and heavily medicated, while resting on the far couch. Even so, he was doing his best to stay tuned in to what was going on, "W-why don't you sit yo drunk ass down and use your brain for a change." He said weakly.

Roscoe squinted his eyes at him, "Mayne you lucky yo big ass is on the injured reserve list right now, otherwise I'da had to go upside your head for that slick ass shit." Ivory turned and smiled, "Yeah well come on wit it, even fucked up I can still handle yo little ass." Roscoe shot him the bird, then stumbled over to the bar seats. "Not to sound dumb or anything, but what's this Muhammad's son have to do with anything?" Gina asked.

"He alone isn't the problem. What Trackz is getting at, is that each of our targets has been a rich or connected black man. Not one target has been white, Indian, or even Latino. Then taking into account how much money we're receiving for taking out our own people, you'd have to assume this is a government funded operation." Skiddlez answered with a hand still on his forehead. "Yes, exactly!" Trackz jumped up, and started pacing the floor as the wheels in his mind started turning in sequence, "Okay, so have ya'll heard of COINTELPRO?"

Without waiting for a response he continued, "It stands for Counter Intelligence Program, and it was created by the FBI. It was mainly targeted on black nationalist groups going back to Elijah Muhammad & Malcolm X days. The way they worked is, they would get people of color to infiltrate these organizations and report back to them. Out of fear of what these radicalistic groups could do with their anti-slavery organizations and equal-ity movements if they got too much power, they took it a step further and used these spies to divide the groups from within.

A simple divide & conquer maneuver, and it worked flaw-lessly every time. Not being able to trust anybody around you, makes it hard to organize and come together to fight a massive force united against you. Using our own people against us goes as far back as how they used Africans to lure their unsuspecting people to the very first slave ships. Today, we simply call people snitches but it's the same just on a grander scale.

Anyways, I digress... Okay so, haven't you ever wondered what happened to the revolutionist? Where's our Freedom Fighters, where's our Martin Luther Kings of our generation, our Fredrick Douglass'? What happened to the Black Panthers, shit what happened to Black Power? The problem is, anytime one of our people gets too much power, or too many followers, while preaching freedom and equality for the oppressed African

Americans, they end up assassinated. Shit look what happened to Tupac.

So my personal opinion is that we're scared and have grown complacent with life as it is, even though our people still have a long way to go to realize our full potential and who we really are. Nevertheless, what worries me now that involves us in particularly, is that we are working for the Feds. The very same inventors of COINTELPRO, and destroyers of all black revolutionist come and past. What worries me worst is that they've raised the stakes, and have just gone to eliminating any of us with money and power. In which case, we are the man's black hit squad for the blacks."

He snapped out of his zone & speech to find everyone's eyes on him and mouths open. Skiddlez was the first to snap out of it, "Are you sure about this Trackz?" He locked eyes wit him, "Bro I don't wanna be, but I'm pretty fuckin sure. This shit's been eating at me from the jump, and now I know why." D-Money grabbed a bottle and took a deep gulp, "Damn my nig, you just blew my high wit dat shit right there. Baby roll a fat one up for me ASAP."

Roscoe lurched from the bar, "Mayne, fuck all that black history shit. Long as we getting paid, what the fuck any of these niggas got to do wit us. Niggaz dyin every day, rich niggaz, broke niggaz, if we don't hit em, somebody else will, so I say if there's a price on they heads then we collect it and move on to the next ones."

Trackz shook his head looking at him sadly, "Now see, that's the problem. That's exactly what they capitalize on. The greed, savageness, and heartlessness that's been shown so far. They play on our ignorance, but tell me this… If rich, successful, & established negroes are expendable and targeted right? What do you think they are going to do to us when they are done with us? You think they gon just let us walk away? The moment we signed up for this… We killed ourselves."

Everyone sat and digested that for a while. All the fight had left Roscoe, reality had finally set in & he slumped down into the couch next to Jo-Jo. "Trackz, get everything you can on our employer and anybody connected. If we're expendable and possible future targets, we're gonna need to make sure we strike first and eliminate anyone who knows about us in their organ-ization." Skiddlez ordered. "Already on it boss..." As the rest of the group got lost in thought about the situation they'd gotten themselves into, the only thing in the room to be heard was the keys of Trackz's laptop.

22

Somewhere across the country a red light turned on... Somewhere else, a computer booted up and began running a protocol... Somewhere aways from there a phone rang. A man wrapped up in the arms of an ebony hooker answered, knowing only one person had that number, already sure of it's purpose. "Flags were raised in the Cyber Defense Department. Seems your little trained monkeys are planning a mutiny." Said the voice on the other end.

"I'll handle it sir." The man's heartbeat was racing. He'd like to believe it was just from all the drugs in his system, but he knew better. The party with the hooker could only account for so much... He knew the truth. "We know you will. Your life depends on it." The man's face grew paler than usual. He sighed knowing this time would come sooner or later. As he sent his good time packing, it was his turn to make a call.

Another phone rings back down south, "Hello?" Baby G answered without looking at the screen. "Le'me find out you done forgot about an old lady already." The voice automatically brought a smile to her face, and she dropped what she was doing. "Hey mama! Now one, you ain't old, and two, I'll never forget about you. Ever."

"Mhm, that's why I ain't heard from you on our regular day. Who is he?" She almost choked on her soda she was drinking, "What you mean who is he? Who is who?" "Girl, don't play with me. You been calling me like clockwork on the same day and time since you left. Then all of a sudden, I hear nothing. Now knowing your lil fast ass, that only means one thing. Not that I mind you finally getting comfortable up there, but who is he?"

Baby G couldn't do nothing but smile. She loved how

much her mother knew her, and that was the best feeling in the world to have that kind of bond with her. "His name's Juice if you must know, and it ain't nothin serious. We just kickin it every now and then." "Juice huh? What he s'posed to be Tupac or something?" She laughed, "That's the same thing I said when I met him." They both laughed this time.

She proceeded to describe him to her, and answer her questions as they fell into their normal rhythms. "So how did you meet this Juice anyway?" "Now that's another interesting story. To sum it up, I met him at work during a robbery. Though it wasn't until..." Recollection suddenly reminded her that she hadn't thought about that day with Lil Mic since it happened. She must have been repressin her feelings or something, because the minute she thought about it, she seemed to be right back in that alley about to be raped.

"Hello... when what... what happened baby... hello..." She came too and her hands were shaking. She got mad at herself for her reaction. The shit must have affected her more than she realized. She always heard about bitches getting raped, but never really thought it would almost happen to her. (Bitch you a gangsta, ain't nobody got time for that.) She thought to herself. She shook it off, and told her mother what had happened, minus the body she left.

Daysia, of course had come into the room, and was now rolling up and listening intently. "He what!? I know this little muthafucka didn't put his hands on my baby! Oh lord, thank God for that young man Juice. Next time you around him, you make sure to call me so I can thank him myself. Now what did you say this little ruffian's name was?"

Baby G could hear the emotion in her mother's voice, then realized she had a tear rollin down her face as well. She immediately switched gears into anger. "Some stupid little nigga that calls himself Lil Mic. He a short, fat, oil black muthafucka, dat ain't got no respect but swear he somebody." There was a pause on the phone.

"Hello, mama? You still there?" After a second, she got a response, "Y-yeah, I'm still here baby. Just the person you described reminded me of someone from the past... What's this boy's last name?" Baby G thought for a second, then asked Daysia. "His name's Boyle mama, why?" She heard the phone drop and a bunch of "Oh Lords" coming from the background. Finally her mama picked the phone back up, and her voice sounded completely different.

"Gabryiana you stay the hell away from that boy. I don't care what you gotta do, but stay away from that boy. I know you probably want yo revenge or whatnot for what he did to you, but you gotta let that go and stay as far away from that boy as possible." She wasn't used to hearing her mother worked up like this, "Mama what are you talking about? What's wrong? You know him or something?"

A funny feeling was starting to come over her. "No, and yes. Baby, I'm gon tell you something, but you gotta promise me you gon stay away from him and not do nothing stupid." "Mama what is it, what's wrong?" "First of all, I'm proud of how good you been doing. You've done real good at keeping yo word, but I want you to quit yo stupid ass job and I don't want you walkin out there alone in them streets anymore. You hear me?"

Baby G was getting more and more worried with every word she spoke. She'd already quit her job, and didn't plan on being out there walkin anymore anyways now that she had Juice. "Okay mama, no problem. Now tell me what's going on. What's wrong?" There was another pause, "Baby I don't know how in the hell, or what cruel joke the Devil is playing with this family... but that little boy who been harassing you, is the son of the dirty muthafucka that set up your father!"

23

Terrance Whitewood, also known as 'The Boss' to Da Squad, had received the call from his superiors about the situation. Apparently, he had some kind of mutiny on his hands with his newest team of hitters. It's to be expected, soon or a later they all figure it out. Though this one put the pieces together allot sooner than his previous teams.

Had to be that little hacker, something told him to watch out for that smart little son of a bitch. Nevertheless, all good things must come to an end. He never grew attached to his little teams. They were like pets to him, and when they got out of line, it was simply time to euthanize them. Now this little group of hounds had grown rabid, and the time had come to lay them to rest.

He'd been through the motions so many times, that he'd almost absently initiated the protocols to get the cleanup squad ready. So he was anticipating the call when it had come in. The leader of their little gang had requested a meetup, to which he agreed to, in some remote location they'd probably thought cleverly concealed their intentions. The little hoodlums were always so predictable.

His people were all over the place concealed & disguised by time he had arrived fashionably late. No way he was gonna just walk up into their little trap, he had been the one to train them. He just always wanted a front seat to the show. It was the least he could do, out of respect, of course. "I'm here, where to now?" He asked coolly through the phone. "Room 232. You came alone right?" Skiddlez replied.

Terrance rolled his eyes at the cliché response, and played his role. "Of course, I'll be up in a sec." Of course he'd already known what room they were in, his team had been clocking them since the moment they'd arrived on scene a hour before.

He double checked through his coms that they were still located & visible. The snipers responded with 100% visibility on each. Pity, it's almost too easy.

Lighting up a cigar, he gave his team the order. Gunfire erupted as Team A eliminated the targets. Terrance gave the signal after a few seconds, and Team B rushed in to confirm and finish the job. The door to 232 was kicked in and more gunshots erupted. The news will show a segment about a drug deal gone wrong, 60 seconds, and all will be forgotten. Good riddance to more street scum. Boo-hoo family & friends, then life goes on.

Terrance made the sign of the cross, then snubbed out his cigar. Jumping in his car, he made the call to the higher ups to inform them all was handled. In his mind he was already putting together his next prospects to be trained. This time no smart alecky hackers he promised himself, and laughed to himself at his own humor.

24

"...the son of the man who set up your father..." Those words reverberated around in her head for a while as her mother continued talking. Daysia, noticing the look on her face, had lit a blunt of loud and passed it to her. When she'd finished the convo with her mother, she had relayed everything she'd learned to her cousin. The whole night had been a blur after that. The words still bounced around her mind as they stood in a gym surrounded by people.

She told her mother she was done wit that job, and she'd meant it. Though now she had to find a new one, or figure out her next step. The only way she could do that was to talk to Mrs. Higgins. Conveniently, there just happened to be a job fair/ Bar-b-cue going on at the school. Daysia, always the optimist, had convinced her to stop through claiming it was a win/win situation. Baby G recalling all her negative encounters with the bitch of a gatekeeper, wasn't so sure.

Still, she had dressed the part & painted the best square smile she could muster up combo'd with a square expression. She doesn't recognize a single face in the crowd, but receives more than a few dirty looks. "Ummm... Are you sure about this Daysia? I'm feeling a little out of place, and to be real if I get one more dirty look from one of these weak ass bitches, I'ma show the fuck out!" She said loud enough for those surrounding to hear, but still held the fake smile plastered on her face.

"Chill cuz, you got this. Ignore them, they just goin off the stories they done heard about you. Just remember, you are what you will to be. Think positive and you'll attract positive things. We're all connected through a energy that flows through all things like electricity. Harness that, visualize what you want, speak it into existence, then believe that it is already yours and it will be." Daysia responded with her usual mentality.

FOR BETTER OR WORSE

"Yeah uh-huh. Whatever you say cuz." She replied, not really understanding anything she'd just said. "Now, where's this ol Sandlot bitch at so we can get this over with, then get the fuck outta here?" They looked for a while, but couldn't spot Mrs. Higgins anywhere. To make good use of her time, Baby G began filling out applications at the booths that interested her.

All the fakeness was wearing down her energy and she wanted nothing more than to smoke a blunt. After a few applications and "We'll call yous." She began to start noticing the same trend booth after booth, "Day, I feel like these people bullshittin me, and just tryna shoo me off." She confessed. Daysia looked at her, then quickly looked away. "Bitch what? Just say it."

Daysia's eyes settled on the floor for a while. "Well... I ain't want you to get discouraged, but they ain't gone do nothing till Mrs. Higgins gives them the go head..." Just like that, the smile dropped from Baby G's face. "Are you fuckin serious right now? You mean to tell me I need this hoe's stamp of approval to even get one of these bullshit muthafuckas to even glance at my application of a muthafuckin minimum wage job fair?! This small-town shit is outta hand. Ain't there laws against monopolizing shit!"

It took everything in her not to slap the shit out of a random person passing by. She breathed deep a couple times, and regained her composure. "Alright, fuck it. Let's just find this bitch so we can get ghost before I catch a charge." Daysia happily agreed, relieved to see her cousin handling things in the proper way for once. "First, I need to stop by the bathroom."

They weaved through the crowd to the rest room. Baby G fixed herself in the mirror as her cousin relieved herself. A few minutes passed and three ghetto fabulous looking females entered. Baby G payed em no attention as two moved through the stalls, but did take note that they didn't go in any of them. Instincts up, she also noticed the third one posted by the door and the distinct sound of the lock clicking, "Ok whatever you hoes got on your mind, I advise you stuff that shit right back down and go bout ya bizness cuz I'm not in the mood for no ratched-ness at the moment."

She continued fixing herself in the mirror, but kept them each locked in her peripherals. "Pheh, get a load of this bitch. It's three of us, and she gon pop off like she runnin shit. Bitch please!" Baby G felt the shift in the atmosphere and dodged right just as a fist flew by her head and connected with the mirror. She twisted her body, and came around with a back slap that sounded through the bathroom. She snatched the bitch up by her weave and came up with a blade to her throat.

The other two stood back speechless, confused at what to do next. The one who appeared to be the leader gave a little nod of the head to the other by the door. Before Baby G could decide whether to off the bitch she held, to get to the next one. Daysia came flying out of the stall with a superman punch to the bitches face, knockin her clean out. Sure she was always on her positive vibe, but she had them hands and wasn't nobody to be fucked wit. Seeing the odds shift, and her crew incapacitated, little Mrs. Ratchet's demeanor changed up.

"So now bitch, would you like to tell me what the fuck ya little problem is?" Baby G stood with her blade still to the first one's throat, damn near drawing blood, while shooting daggers through the wanna be boss bitch. She had the audacity to put on a front and play hard rolling her eyes, "Fuck you, I guess the rumors are true about you, that shit don't scare me though hoe. You need to check ya hoe ass cousin, is what you need to do before I show you how I really get down."

Baby G glanced at Daysia who shrugged her shoulders, "The fuck is you goin on about bitch, you got a problem wit my cousin here?" "No hoe, your other one. The hoe that was at my baby daddy's party on Friday. Bitch think she can be all over my man and get away with it, then she got another thing comin."

Still perplexed, Baby G just stared at her for a second, "You talkin bout Kyra? Bitch please, she already got a man & she ain't no hoe, so I know she wasn't pushin up on whatever lame ass nigga you done trapped into child support. So bye bitch!" The bitch acted like she wanted to do something, so Baby G threw her little hostage to the side and squared up.

Just as she thought, the other one looked around and backed down. Baby G shook her head & laughed, "That's what I thought." Mrs. Ratchet sucked her teeth, "Lil Mic ain't no lame, and I ain't trick him into nothing. I love him, and you need to tell your trifling ass cousin to stay away from him because he's mine." Hearing Lil Mic's name triggered something in her. All she could think of was what her mother had told her.

This nigga had been harassing the shit out of her since she got to town, his father set up her father, the muthafucka tried to rape her, and here was this trash ass bitch standing in front of her claiming him as her baby daddy and that she loved him. She didn't know whether to laugh at her ignorance, or stomp a hole in the bitch as collateral. Before she could make a move, Daysia grabbed her by the shoulders and started pulling her to the door, "Let it go G, she ain't worth it."

Every fiber in her body wanted to jam the blade she was holding through each one of the bitch's eye sockets, but she knew her cousin was right. Instead she turned and glared at her, "Bitch I advise you and Lil Dick watch your backs before ya'll get what you lookin for." With that, her & Daysia left them to lick their wounds and tend to their unconscious homegirl.

"Let's find this bitch Mrs. Higgins, and get the fuck out of here before I end up catching a couple bodies instead of a job." She told Daysia, and they cut back through the crowd. She couldn't shake a thought out of her head though, along with a feeling that was growing in the pit of her stomach. "There's no way Kyra would be at that party... right? And if so... She definitely wouldn't be around Lil Mic... would she?" She thought for a second longer, "Hell naw... at least not of her own free will... she wouldn't," That last thought unsettled her more than anything,

25

Terrance awoke groggily with a searing pain in his side. Disoriented, the next thing he felt was his throbbing headache. It felt like New Years 2000 all over again. He must've drank way too much and blacked out, because he couldn't bring a single memory of the night to mind. He heard the voices coming from the T.V., and it sounded like one of those urban movies.

He realized how sluggish his body was as he willed his eyes to open, and they refused to respond. After a moment, he realized his eyes were open but he saw nothing but black. That wasn't right, no matter how dark his room was, he could always see something. Make out a silhouette, the ceiling, his clock... something. That searing pain ran up his side again, and there was a faint jingling sound in the distance.

He tried to rise and double over, but it proved extremely difficult. On top of that, he couldn't seem to get his arms or legs to respond. Come to think of it... as that jingling sound grew nearer and more frequent, he wondered how in the hell he could hear the T.V. but couldn't see even the faintest light. His first thought was that he'd finally gone and done it, he'd drunken himself blind.

(Good fuckin job buddy, you proud of yourself now?) he asked himself as a slow panic began to rise, his senses began to kick through his disorientation, and his panic increased as the pieces of his condition didn't fit together. As he made another attempt to rise, he realized he was upside down. Also... He wasn't blind, there was something over his head, which would also account for his headache.

He tried to move his hands & feet again, but failed. The constant jingling sound broke through the fog as he struggled, revealing that he was chained up. *Umph* something hard slammed into his ribs knocking the wind out of him. "Wake yo bitch ass up!" came the voice from the T.V... wait, that wasn't the T.V... it was too close, and oddly familiar. "I know you hear me house nigga, we see you moving!"

Oh God, he thought. That definitely wasn't the T.V. Two and two together, his situation became very clear. Somehow, someway, he'd been captured. "Who... Who are you? Why are you doing this? Do you know who your fuckin with?" Escaped his lips before he could stop them. Laughter erupted around him. "Nigga please." Came one voice. "Oh yeah, we definitely know who we fuckin wit." Came another.

"Yeah, an ol Samuel L. Jackson muthafucka." Taunted another, "Yeah, what is dat nigga doin up on dat dere nag?" Imitated another. "Except, right now, you lookin more like you in Django's position." "Yeah, but he damn sure ain't no Jamie Foxx, came a female voice." More laughter. "You think we should add the slave mask, maybe even clip his nuts." "Awww come on bruh, that's going too far." "Really, I don't think nothing's too far for this Benedict Arnold, slave catchin muthafucka." "Aight, everybody shut the fuck up and stop playin wit ya food." Came an extremely familiar voice.

Terrance's heart faltered and then resumed beating rapidly. "Please... I've got money, I'll give you anything you want, just let me go!" He pleaded. Somebody sucked their teeth, "Are you fuckin serious. Cliché much muthafucka. This ain't no movie nigga, you mine-as-well trash the script." Then just like that, the hood was ripped off his head, and his worse fears were confirmed. "Surprise muthafucka!" His eyes grew wide as he focused on his captors.

"Aww, what's wrong? Do you see dead people?" "It damn sure ain't no gift... well not yours atleast." More laughter. "Bu... bu... but how. You're dead, your all dead... I saw..." and as he spoke the words, he found his mistake. His cockiness had come back to bite him in the ass. Instead of staying back and confirming, he'd assumed therefore underestimating his enemies. He'd been doing it for so long that he'd become complacent.

"Since your memory seems to be playing tricks on you, I guess we could help you fill in the blanks as a last request." Skiddlez was standing nose to nose with him, and a cynical grin as he spoke.

-        -

(12 hours earlier) Skiddlez & Ivory sat on one of the hotel beds, staring at six people in a similar room, on a laptop that Trackz set up for them. "You sure this shits gonna work?" Ivory asked with his pistol clutched. Skiddlez nodded, "Positive bruh, trust in yo boi." Ivory just nodded his head, and asked no more questions. If there was anybody in the world he trusted, it was the man sitting next to him.

"He's here." Came Trackz voice over the comm. No sooner than a sniper bullet pierced through the wall blowin the T.V. up. They both dropped to the floor clutching their pistols. More shots rang out, then silence. Footsteps sounded, then the hotel door came crashing in, and semi-to-fully automatic weapons let loose sending bullets through every square inch of the room.

"Clear." The sound of footsteps moved through the room. A body moaned on the ground. *Bam* A single shot to the head put him out of his misery. "Targets eliminated." Skiddlez & Ivory lie on the floor silently watching the scene unfold on the laptop. The volume raised, so they could make out everything being said. Once they heard what they wanted, they waited five minutes before gathering their things and sliding out the room behind 203. With everyone's attention on the other side of the building, they made their way to the vehicle with the rest of the squad undetected.

"Yo DAT shit was CRAYZIE!" said D-Money once they were all in. "Yeah I can't believe that shit actually worked!" said Roscoe. "Damn... that's fucked up. I guess they really do think all black people look alike." Jo-Jo said solemnly. Trackz and Skiddlez looked at each other knowingly. "Yeah mayne, the law is ruthless... but even I didn't think that was gonna work. I gotta admit though, ya'll was right." Ivory confessed dappin up Skiddlez and Trackz, givin em their respect.

Together they had come up with the plan of getting six fiends together to unknowingly play as them. All they had to do was pay for the room, and give em some product to party with. Sure enough the laws saw six black people that 'Fit the description', and without second guessing massacred them. They'd probably release some story about it being gang or drug related, then forget it even happened. Good ol American justice.

"Did ya'll get your part done?" Skiddlez asked. "Yup, he's on the move right now." Trackz answered glancing at the two screens on the dash. One showed the same view of the hotel room Skiddlez & Ivory were watching, and the other showed a dot moving on a map. While Terrance was enjoying his handy work, they had crept up and slipped a tracking device on his car. He had gotten into his vehicle oblivious, and driven off proud of himself.

"Tsk... Tsk... Tsk... And he's supposed to be the brains of this spy shit." Spoke D-Money. They followed the dot until it pulled into the parking lot of a little pub. "This muthafucka ain't waste no time going to celebrate, now did he?" Acknowledged Roscoe. "Yeah, that's something you can relate to bruh. Why don't you go on in and have a couple shots wit him Roscoe? We'll wait." D-Money joked.

"Ha Ha Ha, real funny. You're just a regular comedian, aren't you? Fuck you nigga." Roscoe slurred as D-Money popped his collar and did a lil Bankhead Bounce, "Anyways nigga, what I need some shots for when I got my own bottle." In response he took a big gulp of the bottle of Hennessy he'd been clutching, let out an exaggerated "Ahhh", then laughed at himself. The rest of the squad just shook their heads.

A few hours later, Terrance came out of the pub feeling like a million dollars. He din't have a care in the world as he strutted to his car. He was still whistling a tune when the hypodermic needle was jammed into him and he collapsed into waiting arms.

\-   \-

(Presently) "So, yeah… we brought you to this snazzy lil spot, and used you as a punching bag for a while until you came to." Skiddlez stood with the same sardonic smile, his arms open gesturing to the abandoned warehouse they were in. Terrance was getting lightheaded from all the blood rushing to his head. He was disappointed in himself for being so stupid, and his mind raced to try and find a way out of the fate that awaited him. So Skiddlez next words gave him a glimmer of hope if nothing else.

"No worries, there's still something you can do for us to make things right." "He means the whole deceiving us into killing our own people, then setting us up to be slaughtered in case you weren't sure what needed to be made right." D-Money added, then shrugged his shoulders at the looks everyone gave him. "What, I'm just sayin…" Regardless, Terrance looked up expectantly, "What is it, I'll do almost anything."

Skiddlez cocked his head sideways. "Almost huh?" That's comical, so you actually have some limitations and values in there somewhere. Anyways, it's simple... All you gotta do is tell us where we can find the top dog, the shot caller... your boss & your boss's boss. Everyone who gives the orders all the way up to the top."

Terrance thought for a minute, looked around at the six people, pausing at the two girls, then shook his head. "Nope fuck that, go ahead and kill me. Ain't shit you can do to me compared to what they're capable of. Matta-fact, if that's what you're looking for, then you'll be right behind me anyways. Take my advice. Be happy you got me, and go and live whatever lives you can salvage." There was silence for a second.

"I'll be damned if the lil weasel muthafucka ain't got some type of loyalty in there." Spoke Prissy with mock admiration. "Yeah, or he's just a scared lil bitch... My money's on the lil bitch option." D-Money tagged. Skiddlez gave the signal, and Ivory &

Roscoe dragged a barrel over and placed it under Terrence. "Bad choice my wayward brother." Trackz sympathized.

The lid was removed revealing the three quarters full liquid of hydrofluoric acid that awaited. "Shoulda been more worried about your immediate threat, as opposed to your future phantom ones. Cooperation would have earned you a bullet to the head. Instead, you chose the slow disintegration route. Those bad choices in life is what led you to this position in the first place..." Just as he was about to give the signal, a phone started ringing.

Terrance's head dropped, he recognized that ring anywhere. It was the one that always made his heart double-time, and drop everything. "Well well well, speak of the Devil." Skiddlez said seeing the words "Boss" on Terrance's screen, "Now what I think you failed to realize, is that my boi right here is a beast wit dis tech shit. The only reason your systems were alerted to his presence, was because he allowed it. Everyone it touched to get you, he been trackin. Your phone just gave us the

ANDREW BETHEL

last link. All the dominoes is lined up, you're the first in a chain reaction, and the effect is gonna cause each and every one of ya'll to fall."

He gave the signal and Ivory grabbed hold of the rope holding Terrance up. "Simply put... Ya'll fucked wit the wrong niggas." Ivory growled into his ear just before slow dipping him into the barrel up to his forehead. His blood curdling screams were music to his ears. He let him sit like that as the acid ate up his hair and skin, and seeped to the bone, then he pulled him back out.

He smiled sinisterly at him as he screamed and cried, begging for mercy. He continued to play with him as the rest of the squad stood back watching. Nobody blinked, nobody spoke a word. Gina & Prissy stood tough arm in arm with their men, showing not a hint of squeamishness. Prissy even had a half smile on her face. Da Squad stood enjoying the show until finally the screams stopped from his body going into shock.

Ivory frowned, disappointed that it didn't last longer. Regretfully he lowered the rest of the body into the barrel and allowed the acid to do the rest. He looked at Skiddlez and nodded. They knew what this meant. The game was on, the big brass will put two and two together & they'll be sending everything they got after them.

That was fine wit Da Squad, because they planned on hitting them long before they see anything coming. Just like Terrence, their arrogance will be their downfall. They were fighting for more than just their lives now. They were making a stand, and fighting back for every African American and minority's life that the government deemed expendable. The revolution has begun.

26

"I don't see that bitch nowhere Day, and I'm really starting to feel like some fuck it shit. This ain't even me anyways, I'd feel better goin back and finding Lil Dick's baby mama & showin her how real bitches get down." Baby G fumed after looking every-where inside the school for Mrs. Higgins, but coming up empty handed. She had been trying her best, but that confrontation in the bathroom was becoming harder to walk away from the more the seconds passed.

"Chill G, remember why you're doing this. You got a promise to keep, and you been doing a great job so far. Don't let some triflin ass, nobody, hoodrats take that away from you. As for Mrs. Higgins, she's around here somewhere, trust. When there's events like this, she's never far away so she can throw her weight around. The best things to do, are usually the hardest to get accomplished. All these obstacles just mean your doing the best things for your life, & the enemy is working over time to trip you up. Stay positive, picture what you want, and go get it."

Daysia flipped her hair, "Now smile bitch, and let's go find the only person standing in your way." Baby G couldn't do anything but shake her head at her cousin, and smile. That's why she loved her, because she was always trying to see the light at the end of the tunnel. They searched for another 10 minutes with no results. Her legs were starting to get tired, so Daysia suggested they go outside by the football field and rest on the bleachers.

Low and behold, the moment they stepped out on the track, they spotted a small group standing a little ways off. The strong smell of barbecue wafted towards them in the smoke, as a chubby old school manned the grill. "Of course, things are always where you least expect em. Popping up right when you stop looking for em, and notoriously in the last place you look."

Daysia commented.

Centered in the small group, stood Mrs. Higgins demanding the attention of those around. Baby G & Daysia waited patiently on the outside of the circle, until the proper opportunity arrived. "Um... excuse me, Mrs. Higgins, could we please have a moment of your time?" Daysia spoke up in her most polite voice. The fake smile she'd been wearing faltered as soon as her eyes set on Baby G. She looked back and forward between the two, seeming undecided.

Quickly recovering, she continued her spiel with the remaining three people around her. Once she'd seemed to sell whatever scheme she was selling, she turned to the two, her smile absent completely & nose now turned in the air. "What do you want?" She directed her question at Baby G.

Taken aback for a second by the cold response, she just stood there staring back at her. Daysia quickly intervened, "Well we were filling out applications in the job fair, and knew that it would only be respectable to approach you and run some opportunities by you, ma'am." The fake smile and air of superiority returned as she looked at Daysia. "Of course dear, you know anything you want I'll be more than happy to check into for you." Daysia smiled at that, and Baby G began to relax a little.

Then the coldness returned just as quickly, "But not for her." She said the "her" as if she were disgusted at the sudden sight of a mouse in her dinner. Baby G was tired of the disrespect, and found her voice. "Look, I don't know what your problem is with me, or what you heard, but I can promise you that I don't want any trouble. I'm trying to do the best thing for my life.

I have allot of skills for qualifications in multiple positions, and I know if given the chance I'd be a huge asset to whatever company I joined. I'm a fast learner & very hard worker, and I know I can thrive in any position. All I need is you to allow me to get my foot in the door to prove it... ma'am." Baby G took a deep breath after the words came tumbling out.

She'd given the most respect she could muster up, and sold herself to the best of her abilities. Her voice had matched the polite one that Daysia had gotten such a positive response from, while wearing her most innocent face. To her & Daysia's surprise, Mrs. Higgins looked as if somebody had slung shit into her face, "I DON'T like you. You ain't shit, and never gone be shit. Your part of the problem. I've heard and seen it all before. You say you wanna change, but never will. I refuse to waste my time and resources on a lost cause! Now if you'll excuse me, I have some real business to attend to."

With that, she rolled her eyes and walked off. Baby G & Daysia stood rooted to their spots, stunned by the whole ordeal. So many thoughts and emotions ran through Baby G's head. (Well... There you go. You gave it your best shot. Nobody can blame you for anything you do after this.) She thought, on one hand, she wanted to stomp a mud hole in the smug bitch's face. Then on the other, she couldn't seem to comprehend what the bitch's problem was.

"I can't believe she just... Uh-uh, hell no G. You ain't gotta take that, come on let's try and talk some sense into her..." Daysia said exasperated. Baby G held her hand up to stop her, and shook her head. She began to walk off, not checking if Daysia was following or not. Daysia raised her voice, "That ain't right. The older people who can help, have given up on the youth. So when they are trying to change, instead they are belittled and turned away. Everybody has potential to be great, and nobody should be denied a second shot. She's wrong for treating you like that. Nobody should be judged off of rumors, their looks, or other people's mistakes. Then if you've taken responsibility for the mistakes you have made, you should be given the tools to turn over a new leaf. She's just written you off for who she thinks you are. THAT'S NOT RIGHT!!!"

Tears were flowing from her eyes, and her voice had risen to it's highest octaves. Everyone's attention was on her as she made her speech. Everyone except Mrs. Higgins, who tried to pretend like she was in a deep conversation with the parents of a child. Though she acted like she hadn't heard a word, she heard the whole thing. Daysia caught up with Baby G, who'd seemed to be walking in a daze.

"Hol' up cuz. You aight?" She just shook her head and kept drifting through the crowds. She was still trying to wrap her head around what went wrong. The way Mrs. Higgins talked to her, showed that she didn't have the slightest chance in getting a decent job or anything around there. She just couldn't understand. She'd been doing everything right that she possibly could, yet around every corner some bullshit stayed lurking.

Doors just kept slamming in her face. So the fuck was she supposed to do? How did her mother expect her to do the right thing, when everyone was fucking off. "Come on G, let's take a walk. I know the perfect place to calm down." Daysia led her out of the school. They walked in silence for a good 10 minutes, both stuck in their thoughts. "Over here." Daysia finally spoke. They came up on a large abandoned high school. "This is the high school all of our parents went to, and all the legends of the hood."

They went through a side gate that led through a big field around the back. She stopped at a big wall that connected to the outside of the gym. "Every legend's name used to be tagged back here. All the big shots, and their crews. The OGs, and their ride or die bitches. The graffiti and memorials used to make it all look like a beautiful piece of art." Baby G looked up at the wall confused.

Daysia read her face, "The stupid young-ins recently painted over it all, them being the new legends. Then they disrespectfully tagged their names on the clean slate." Sure enough the wall now held nothing but dumb ass names she'd never heard of. All except one, Lil Mic's name sat listed with some of the stupid muthafuckas in his squad.

Daysia pulled out a pre-rolled and they sat down to smoke it. As the pot leaf took effect, Baby G's mind took off on the stipulations of her situation. It was here she decided she was gonna change things one way or another, for better or worse. Daysia's phone rang, snapping them both out of it.

"Hey mom... WHAT!?..." She now had Baby G's full attention. "Oh my God, is she alright?" Fresh tears sprung from Daysia's eyes. Baby G kept asking what was going on, but was getting no response. After the emotional conversation, she finally hung up. With rivers flowing down her face, she turned to Baby G, "Oh my God G, Kyra's in the hospital!"

Baby G felt like she'd been punched in the gut, "What, why, what's wrong with her?" Daysia shook her head. "My mom said, she was found Saturday morning by some jogger. She was raped and badly beaten. She's in a coma, and in critical condition." It felt like all the air in her body had been removed.

They cried together for a while holding each other. Her eyes glanced over the wall, and something clicked. "Wait a second... You remember what that bitch said in the bathroom? She said Kyra was going into a room with Lil Mic. That was Friday night. I knew something didn't sound right about that shit." The tears had stopped and were now replaced with a burning rage.

"You don't think..." Daysia started. "I don't think cuz, I fuckin know it. I can feel it in my gut. That twisted little muthafucka tried to do the same thing to me. He must've taken it out on Kyra as retaliation." That was it, she felt a shift inside of her.

"Fuck it then. Pussy nigga wanna play, I'ma show em how to really rock out. I'm done playing by these lame ass rules, tryna live a square's life. That shit ain't me. These niggas done fucked wit me, now they done touched my cousin. Now I'ma have to touch each and every one of em. I'ma show em how to lock some shit down. They gone find out what the seed of a true legend is made of."

She clowned the dumb ass names on the wall, spit flying from her mouth as she went into a frenzy over the pain of her cousin. She found a can of paint tossed by the bleachers, and sprayed a 'X' through Lil Mic and his lil fuckbois' names. Then in big broad letters tegged her name, on one of the clean spots, to put everyone on notice that a new player in the game had arrived.

The wheels were already turning full speed in her head. She saw the chess board clearly, and as her first move, she had a few calls she needed to make. The city was about to rain blood. By the time she was done, they'd need to build a whole new cemetery to bury their dead.

-           -

A car sat off in the distance. The driver held a pair of binoculars to his eyes. "A promise is a promise. You've kept me waiting too long. I told you I'd find you, and here you are. Soon my love, we'll be together again. This time, no one will ever separate us again." He watched as Baby G tagged the wall, then kicked up some dirt.

He'd been following her for a couple days now. He would have shown himself, but he was waiting for the right time. He'd only caught her alone walking once, and some lil knuckleheads had intervened right when he was about to pull up on her. "No matter Baby, It's all about timing. Until then... I'll be watching."

To Be Continued...